GOOD AS DEAD

A MATT GAMBLE THRILLER BOOK 1

GARY WINSTON BROWN

This is a work of fiction. Names, characters, places, and incidents – and
their usage for storytelling purposes – are crafted for the singular purpose
of fictional entertainment and no absolute truths shall be derived from the
information contained within. Locales, businesses, companies, events,
government institutions, law enforcement agencies and private or
educational institutions are used for atmospheric, entertainment and
fictional purposes only. Furthermore, any resemblance or reference to
persons living or dead is used fictitiously for atmospheric, entertainment
and fictional purposes.

Cover art and design: Taherul

This book is dedicated to my beautiful wife, Fiona.
I'm lucky to have you in my life and in my corner.

ILYBBOBKS...ATS

1

Distance To Target

THE SHORE CURVED inward along California's Big Sur coastline and provided the owners of the multimillion-dollar mansions perched atop its cliff stunning views of the Pacific Ocean. Matt Gamble had spent the last two days occupying the top floor of one such property. The mansion was owned by a globetrotting billionaire with a passion for flipping high end real estate who had been called out of the country to attend a family emergency. News agencies reported that his brother had launched his Ferrari off a cliff and crashed it on the rocks below, killing him instantly. To the world, it had been a horrific and tragic accident. Gamble knew better. The man's demise was no accident. It was by design, orchestrated, a necessary distraction to ensure that the owner of the mansion in which he had now taken up a position would not be returning for at least the next few days. An Agency technician had been tasked with hacking the Ferrari's software, then taking control of the luxury automobile via a secure satellite link through his laptop. The terrified driver had tried unsuccessfully to fight the steering wheel when suddenly it left his control and took on a life of its own. It was only a matter of time before the inevitable occurred. The technician wove the Ferrari through traffic at breakneck speed. At the exact second when he sent it crashing through the wooden guardrail he terminated the satellite uplink and returned control of the car to its doomed driver. Days earlier, Gamble had received a text informing him that the diversion had been a success and the man had been terminated. It was his turn now.

He was in play.

Gamble stared at his target through the scope of his sniper rifle. Abdel Gutierrez lounged poolside at his stately home two miles away on the opposite side of the cliff. A one-time valued American government asset, the former arms dealer turned legitimate businessman had outlived his usefulness, or so it had been determined by those in the Central Intelligence Agency whose job it was to manage such matters. The information he had to trade for his new life in America and his foreign connections had become outdated and no longer of interest to the powers that be. But it was the knowledge he carried in his head that posed the greatest threat. Names. Dates. Deals. Exchanges. He knew where the proverbial bodies were buried. It was for those reasons and more that Matt had been ordered to end his life.

The setting sun painted the flat surface of the target's pool a burnt orange. Gutierrez had already finished one glass of Scotch. Ten minutes from now, he would pour himself a second. Unlike the first drink, which he sipped and savored, the second was always consumed quickly and impatiently. Matt knew this because he had been watching and noting everything about the man's daily routine since he had arrived in the vacant mansion. Nothing had been left to chance. He had taken a position in the upstairs bedroom to execute the hit. When his mission was completed, he would leave no evidence of his presence behind. When the time came to exfiltrate the premises, the Camoshield clothing he wore would ensure that his near-infrared and thermal infrared signature would be undetectable to the security cameras installed at this and virtually every other property in the area. The technical material of the confusion camouflage suit was multilayered, its many shapes and shades specifically designed to blend in with the rocks and trees of the surrounding landscape and make him nearly impossible to spot. For all intents and purposes, he would be invisible.

Gutierrez downed the second Scotch, stood, dove into the pool, resurfaced seconds later.

Matt had provided his handler with the termination window. High above in the sky, an CIA-piloted drone reached his position. Director Ferriman was looking down now, watching and waiting. The communications earwig in Matt's ear crackled to life. Ferriman spoke to him. "We have your position. Sitrep."

Matt checked the weapon and scope again. He was intimately familiar with how it performed and how the bullet's flight path would behave when distance and external ballistic conditions such as wind, humidity, temperature, barometric pressure, air density, and the curvature and rotation of the Earth were taken into consideration. He knew this because he had sent thousands of practice rounds downrange before under conditions far more challenging than this assignment. From this distance, the wind speed and direction coming off the Pacific Ocean were most important since they could change the trajectory of the bullet while in flight without warning. An American flag hanging slack on its pole on a property nearly a mile away provided a suitable distance indicator and confirmed the conditions. Matt prepared himself, slowed his breathing, waited to find the natural pause that would tell him he was ready to fire the weapon. In the distance, the target was stationary. He provided Ferriman with the situation report he had requested. "Green to go."

"Then what are you waiting for?"

The comment irritated Matt. It had taken him twenty minutes to set up the shot. "What's the rush?" he replied.

"Don't get smart, Gamble," Ferriman said. "Take him now."

"Whose finger is on the trigger, yours or mine?"

"As far as you're concerned, they're one and the same."

"Not from where I'm positioned."

The CIA director was insistent. "This has to get done, Gamble."

"It will."

"Are you forgetting that I can see your distance to target?" Ferriman said. "Your conditions are optimal. Your sightline is unobstructed. Take the fucking shot."

Matt stared at Gutierrez through the scope as he floated on his back on the calm water, enjoying the warmth of the dying sun, oblivious to the fact that his life was about to end. A sudden spray of water splashed across his face. He smiled, flipped onto his stomach, kicked forward. Matt eased the rifle a fraction of an inch to the right, looked for the reason for his target's reaction, saw it. His finger flew off the trigger. "Mission compromised," he announced. "I'm aborting."

"What are you talking about?" Ferriman barked.

"Gutierrez' kid is in the pool with him."

"So?"

"I'll find another time."

"There is no other time, Gamble. Kid or no kid, you have your orders."

"You know my rules, Director. Sanctioned targets only, and never in the presence of a child."

"To hell with your rules! You'll do what I tell you to do. I'm giving you a direct order. Take out Gutierrez now!"

"No."

"What did you say?"

"I'm not about to splatter the kid with his father's brains," Matt replied. He withdrew the rifle, pulled it back into the room, closed the window.

Ferriman watched the rifle barrel disappear into the mansion. "You shouldn't have done that, Matt," he said.

"I don't care."

"There'll be repercussions," Ferriman warned.

"Are you threatening me?"

"I'm stating the facts."

"You don't want to make an enemy of me, sir," Matt replied. "That would be a mistake."

"Now who's making threats?"

"Goodbye."

"Hang up on me and you'll be crossing a line you won't be able to uncross."

"I'll take my chances."

"Do you know what this means for you?"

"I have a pretty good idea."

"The world is a small place, especially for us. There's nowhere you'll be able to hide. We *will* find you."

"Yeah? Good luck with that."

Matt removed the earwig, dropped it on the floor beside him, stomped on it, shattered it to pieces.

In the distance, the target and his son splashed and played.

Matt broke down the Lobaev DXL-5 Havoc sniper rifle, returned the components to its Camoshield covered case, then waited twenty minutes until he felt confident that the drone which had been monitoring his position no longer occupied the airspace above him.

He knew Ferriman had already placed a call. Wheels had been set in motion. Operatives would be assigned to come after him. Of that, he was certain.

He checked his watch. Twenty minutes had passed.

Outside, dusk had transitioned to darkness.

Matt exited the mansion, returned the Havoc to its hidden compartment in the trunk of the specially outfitted Cadillac Escalade, then slowly pulled out of the driveway.

He had one stop to make. After that, he would execute his emergency exfiltration plan and disappear.

The safe house waited.

CENTRAL INTELLIGENCE AGENCY
LANGLEY, VIRGINIA

FERRIMAN TAPPED on his supervisor's office door, waited.

"Come."

He entered the room. "It's been confirmed, sir," he said. "Total mission failure."

Task Force Chief Cameron Cross looked up. "Who is the operative?"

"Matt Gamble. Code name Reaper."

"Circumstances?"

"He disobeyed a direct order."

"Meaning?"

Ferriman paused. "Reaper had a lock on the target, but he refused to take the shot. Gutierrez' son was with him."

"Do we still have an open window on Gutierrez?"

"No, sir. The family is already en route to LAX. Their jet leaves for Honduras within the hour."

"And Reaper?"

"He cut off communication. He's gone dark."

"Very well," Cross said. "Notify all stations. Reaper is now an alpha one priority target. Check everywhere... bus terminals, train stations, airlines, toll cams, police observation devices, the works. I want him found."

"Yes, sir."

"One more thing. Run his profile through predictive analysis. Find out where he's most likely to go, then activate our local assets. I want him put down on sight."

Ferriman nodded. "Right away, sir."

2

No Joy

FERRIMAN PICKED UP the phone and spoke to the drone pilot seated hundreds of miles away behind his command console in a secret CIA Special Operations Center. "Do we still have him?" he asked.

The pilot studied the computer screen in front of him. "No joy, sir," he replied. "The drone has left the airspace."

"Can you redirect?"

"Yes, sir," the pilot acknowledged. He eased the joystick to the left. High above the clouds, the drone changed course.

"How long until we're back on target?"

"Fifteen minutes, sir."

"Damn it!" Ferriman replied. "Do we have another bird in the area we can deploy?"

"Negative, sir."

"All right. Reach out to me the second you have eyes on."

"Copy that."

Ferriman disconnected the call. He knew Reaper, knew his reputation for being the best operative the agency had ever trained, and that there was no way he would still be on target when the drone reached his last known position. The window of opportunity to assassinate Gutierrez had been lost. Matt would have to answer for that. Darkness had now fallen. He thought about his options. He could order a drone strike on Gutierrez's vehicle as it made its way to the airport. In doing so, the missile would vaporize the vehicle and its occupants. The agency could try to spin it, explain it away as a horrific explosion, a fuel leak, perhaps. But there would be other vehicles on the road. Which meant collateral damage in the form of civilian lives lost, not to mention surviving witnesses, some perhaps with military experience who would know a drone strike with absolute certainty when they saw it. Such an act would conjure up a political shit storm which would be impossible to explain away as anything other than what it truly was: the sanctioned deployment of military ordnance and the deliberate assassination of a foreign national on American soil. The Oval Office would be accountable. The presidency itself put in jeopardy. Taking such an action would likely land him in a military prison for the rest of his life. He quickly dismissed the idea and returned his attention to dealing with what his superior had asked him to do: find and eliminate Matt Gamble.

He knew this would be no simple task. The agency would be going after one of their own. Gamble was out there somewhere doing exactly what his government had spent millions of dollars training him to do. Blend in. Disappear. Become a ghost, invisible to the enemy. For the moment, that is precisely what he was.

A ghost.

And now an enemy.

Ferriman's phone rang. He took the call. "Go."

The drone pilot was on the line. "I have an update, sir."

"Yes?"

"I reviewed the video footage the drone recorded before it left the target area. The last two seconds show a vehicle pulling out of the estate. A Cadillac Escalade, black. I can send you the feed if you'd like."

"Do it."

"Sending it now."

Ferriman received the file, reviewed it. "That's him," he said. "What else do we have?"

"Nothing, sir. That's all the bird could capture. Do you want us to continue searching the area?"

"Yes. Notify me the second you've located that vehicle."

"Copy that."

3

Unit 12

THE SAN DIEGO safe house was not a house at all but a vacant auto body repair shop with white-washed windows in a run-down commercial district on the outskirts of the city. Most of the surrounding businesses served the auto trade and provided services ranging from tire sales and transmission repair to emissions testing and custom detailing. This shop was one of many in the auto strip mall. Matt had leased Unit 12 for several reasons. It was the largest unit, was located at the back of the mall, and featured an extra wide steel roll up door. The rear of the property backed on to another commercial complex, the two separated by an eight-foot-high concrete wall. The four forty-five-gallon steel drums and wooden pallets sitting at the foot of the wall directly across from the roll up door appeared to have been left there as refuse. This was not the case. Matt had filled the drums with heavy rocks and placed them there for a reason. If suddenly he had to abandon the unit, he could use them to help him get up and over the dividing wall in four seconds. He knew this because he had timed himself in a flat-out run from the door to the wall. In the event he was pinned down and taking fire, the oil drums would protect him. Like the shop's interior walls and roll up door, Matt had spray coated the inside of each drum with BallistiCrete, a bulletproof plaster capable of offering ballistic protection against everything from a handgun round to an armor piercing bullet.

Per his usual reconnaissance, Matt drove around the complex first, checking out the neighboring units and the vehicles parked in front of them, searching for anything that looked or felt out of place. Over the years he had executed covert missions on four continents. His instincts, and his ability to trust his gut, had been responsible for keeping him alive in some of the most inhospitable places on the planet under the most harrowing of circumstances. He slowed the Escalade on the third pass as he approached the unit. Other than the sounds of pneumatic air wrenches in use in neighboring shops, the revving of car engines, and metal instruments banging on steel, all of which were common for the area, the auto repair mall was relatively quiet. Matt stopped the Escalade in front of the roll up door, exited the vehicle, looked around.

All clear.

The front entrance doorknob looked normal but was anything but. Its two-step biometric anti-intrusion security feature first required the confirmation of Matt's thumb print. He placed his thumb atop the steel knob, then gripped it with his hand. His biometric signature was accepted. The lock released. Matt entered the shop, closed the auto-locking door behind him, walked to the rear of the facility, pressed a button on the wall. The steel roll up door rose slowly, then locked in place. Matt stepped outside, slipped behind the wheel of the Escalade, then backed it into the shop where it would remain until he needed it next, then lowered the door. He returned to the shop's front office, removed a notebook computer from the floor safe located under the plastic mat beneath the desk chair, powered up the device. With a few clicks, he accessed the specially designed software he had purchased from the dark web, hacked into the SUV's satellite navigation system, entered a destination... Bend, Oregon... and pressed ENTER. The black-market software activated. Within seconds, the Escalade was back on the road. Not physically, or course, but virtually. As far as any computer monitoring system could detect, the vehicle was not sitting stationary in the auto garage but was in motion and traveling northbound on Interstate 5. It would continue to follow a phantom route until it reached its algorithmically programmed destination.

Satisfied that the vehicle's GPS and satellite navigation systems were no longer of concern, Matt returned his attention to the safe. Together with the burner phone he kept for emergencies such as this, he removed an electronic keycard, a SIG Sauer P365 9mm handgun, two ten-round magazines, a folding SOG pocketknife, five hundred dollars in twenties, a Rolex Cosmograph Daytona wristwatch, a 24K gold coin ring, and a fake passport capable of passing the closest scrutiny of any airport security agency in the world. He pocketed the phone, money, passport, and keycard, fastened the watch to his wrist, then slipped on the ring. The money was for payoffs. Information was a valuable commodity, but it always came at a price. The watch and ring, each worth tens of thousands of dollars, were bargaining chips. Nothing could secure an off-the-books private plane and shady pilot faster than trading a thirty-thousand-dollar Rolex for time, fuel, and confidentiality. The ring was of equal value and served the same purpose.

In the corner stood a metal locker. Matt walked to it, placed his palm on its integrated biometric scanning pad, waited for the door to open, removed several garments, tossed them onto a chair beside the locker, then closed and locked the door. He removed his shirt, slipped into the ballistic base layer compression vest, put his shirt back on, fitted the gun into the small of his back, the knife into his back pocket, then pulled on the BulletBlocker lightweight flight jacket. The tradecraft garment was capable of stopping rounds ranging from 9mm to .44 Magnum from the front, side, and rear. The BBL compression vest provided additional backup and peace of mind.

It was time to leave.

Matt opened the front door, then waited. Satisfied all was clear, he jogged to the back of the building, jumped the concrete wall, and entered the neighboring industrial complex.

He had one more stop to make.

As he walked along the street, the sky above him turned dark. Storm clouds grumbled. Rain fell. Fat drops splattered on the ground.

Matt cinched his collar tightly around his neck.

For now, he was safe and alive.

He just had to stay that way for the next twenty minutes.

4

A Favor For A Friend

AFTER LEAVING THE industrial complex, Matt stayed off the main roads and followed the neighborhood alleyways until he reached his destination, Hutchinson's Self Storage. He entered the office, found the proprietor seated behind the reception desk, feet up and head down, thoroughly engrossed in a novel.

"Good book?" Matt asked.

The man raised a finger, kept reading. "One sec," he replied.

Matt waited patiently.

Finally, the man turned down the corner of the page to mark where he had stopped reading. "Yeah," he said. "Nobody writes a thriller better than..." He looked up, saw Matt standing in front of him. "Holy shit!" he said. "Matt?"

Matt smiled. "Hi, Hutch."

Peter Hutchinson grabbed his cane, stepped out from behind the reception counter. The former professional hockey player wrapped his arms around him, gave him a fierce hug. "Jesus, Matt. How the hell are you?"

"I'm good. You and Connie?"

"Fine, thanks to you." He stepped back. "Damn, it's good to see you again!"

"Likewise."

Hutch sensed the reservation in Matt's voice. "I take it this isn't a social call."

"I'm afraid not."

"What do you need? Name it and it's yours."

"I need to access my unit."

"You've got it," Hutch said. He walked to the front door, locked it, flipped over the business hours sign from OPEN to BACK IN 15 MINUTES. "Follow me."

Peter and Matt walked through the maze of outdoor storage units until they reached Matt's private unit. "Here she is," Hutch said. "Just as you left her."

Matt removed the electronic key card he had taken from the auto repair shop safe from his pocket, inserted it into the wall mounted reader, then swiped the card. A second device, similar in appearance to a smart doorbell camera, was integrated into the door frame at eye level above the card reader. Matt leaned forward, stared into the camera lens. A synthesized voice spoke through its speaker: "Retinal identification confirmed. Awaiting voice authentication."

Matt spoke: "Reaper."

"Verified," the voice announced. The LED light above the lens changed from red to green. A whirring sound followed as the integrated vault-style bolts successfully disengaged.

Hutch smiled. "I gotta say, Matt. I like your style. This is one sweet system you had built."

Matt's drive in storage unit was unnumbered and did not appear on any of the facility's architectural or engineering drawings, nor was it part of the complex's original design. For all intents and purposes, it did not exist.

"Thanks," Matt said. "I appreciate you allowing me to have it constructed here."

"Are you kidding me?" Hutch said. "I'd let you build ten of them if you wanted to. You never have to thank me. If it wasn't for you intervening when you did, Connie and I would be dead now. You saved our lives. We'll owe you for that until the day we die."

Three years ago, Matt had made Hutch and Connie's acquaintance quite by accident in a Las Vegas back alley when he spied the couple on their knees and begging for their lives, looking up into the eyes of Amadeus Carlotta, one of Sin City's most ruthless debt recovery enforcers, and the two henchmen accompanying him. Matt had been walking past the alleyway, recognized Hutch for the star goaltender he was, then stumbled into the alley, acting as though he was drunk and looking for a place to relieve himself. When he started making a fuss over recognizing Hutch and asking for his autograph and to take a picture together, Carlotta and his men presented their weapons and told him to leave. Matt shuffled up to Carlotta, fell onto the man, laughed, stepped back, slurred an apology, then quickly pulled his silencer-fitted weapon from the cross-draw holster hidden beneath his jacket and put a round between the eyes of the three men before they could react. The bodies collapsed to the ground in unison. Matt quickly covered Connie's mouth as she screamed, told her not to be scared, that it was over now, and that they were safe. With Connie clearly in shock and to ensure they were out of danger, he escorted the couple back to their penthouse suite in the Bellagio Hotel. After Hutch had put his distraught wife to bed, he sat down with Matt and explained the circumstances which had led to their predicament. A high stakes betting consortium had approached him and offered him twenty million dollars to throw the upcoming Stanley Cup final game. He had refused. The mob boss who ran the country's largest illegal gambling site had taken offense to Hutch's refusal to accept his offer. He had tasked Carlotta and his men with changing his mind. When Connie pleaded with him not to kill them, Carlotta responded by slapping her in the face. It was witnessing this action that forced Matt to intervene and simultaneously end both the assault on the couple and the lives of their attackers. Peter gave Matt his cell phone number and told him if he ever needed anything not to hesitate to call. Later, when Connie felt well enough to travel, the couple checked out of the hotel, hit the road, and drove five hundred miles until they reached the California coast and Big Sur. With Connie safely tucked away in the bed-and-breakfast Peter had found, he left his wife and did the only thing he could. He found a section of Pacific Coast Highway 1 which was in need of repair and estimated the distance to the bottom of the cliff. When no other cars were in sight and the opportunity presented itself, he drove his Lexus Q45 SUV off the road, over the cliff, and bailed out the driver's door as the car took flight. As his body rolled down the embankment, he achieved his objective. He broke his leg in the fall, shattered his kneecap, and put an end to his professional hockey career. The incident was reported as a tragic accident, but

Peter knew the truth. No longer could his skills as an athlete be used against him to threaten his family. The relief he felt from this realization far outweighed the months of painful rehabilitation and physical therapy that followed. Years of playing pro hockey had already made him a very rich man. Now it was time to slow down, take it easy. The public storage rental business provided him with an opportunity to do just that. When Matt later learned about his new business venture he reached out to him, told him of his requirement to have the unit built, and that it needed to be kept totally off the books. Hutch was more than happy to accommodate his request.

Hutch leaned on his cane, turned to Matt. "That's a weird name for a code," he said. "Why 'Reaper'?"

"Football," Matt lied. "It was my old high school nickname. I played a pretty rough game."

Hutch smiled. "As in the Grim Reaper."

"Something like that."

Hutch laughed. "I've probably asked too many questions already. God knows the last thing these busted up knees need is for you to tackle *me*. I like walking... such as it is." He looked around the corner. A vehicle had pulled into the visitor parking area. "You gonna be okay from here, Matt?" he asked.

Matt nodded. "I'm good. Go take care of business."

"All right. If you need me for anything, you know what to do, right?"

"I do."

"Take care of yourself, Matt. I'll miss you."

"You too, Hutch."

Matt waited until Hutch had reached the electronic gate, then rolled up the door. The old Ford Econoline delivery van parked inside was dark brown and otherwise unspectacular in appearance. The yellow lettering stenciled on its side panels and rear doors were for a company that did not exist: Perfect Window Cleaning. Its nondescript appearance and business name had been carefully considered so that the vehicle would be easily overlooked in any city or rural setting. Matt opened the door, lowered the sun visor. The vehicle's ignition key fell into his hand. He pocketed the keys, then walked to the mechanic's tool chest located in the back corner of the unit. He opened the twenty-six drawers of the five-bank rolling cabinet one by one and inspected their contents. The three extra wide drawers at the top of the cabinet accommodated his disassembled sniper rifles and assault weapons. The remaining drawers contained everything he would ever need for the completion of a mission: handguns, smoke and concussion grenades, military rifles and scopes, spare ammunition and clips, night vision equipment, an assortment of knives, some for throwing and others for close quarter battle, extra ballistic tactical clothing and footwear, plus several prepaid burner phones and an Iridium satellite phone. He opened the side door of the specially outfitted van, selected the weapons and tradecraft tools he would need, stored them in a metal chest behind the driver's seat, then closed the door. He drove the van out of the storage unit, then secured and locked the unit.

When he reached the gate, he glanced at the front office. Hutch looked up, waved.

He had made it. Now it was time to put as much distance between himself and his current location as possible.

New York City awaited.

5

Dishwasher Needed

EN ROUTE TO New York City, Matt avoided toll roads and interstate highways, opting instead to follow side roads through small towns and rural hamlets. He did this in order to stay off the Agency's radar, which he now assumed would have activated every asset at its disposal to find him. He looked up periodically, searched the sky for signs of surveillance aircraft or the reflection of a high-altitude drone, saw none. Although the journey was indirect, long, and tedious, it was strategically necessary. There was far less of a chance that traffic cameras would capture his vehicle's license plate in these out of the way locales. He kept his speed within posted limits to avoid being caught in police radar traps or detained by a too eager and overly inquisitive small town cop. He drove through the night until he was tired, stopping to sleep for a few hours at a time. Each time he rested he found an out of the way place to hide. First, inside a dilapidated old barn. Next, the bay of an abandoned car wash which had been slated for demolition. Several days later he reached his destination, pulled into the garage of his alternate safe house in Soundview in The Bronx, entered the home, climbed the stairs to his second-floor bedroom, fell onto the bed, and slept for twelve hours straight. When at last he woke it was with a start. In the dream, which had seemed all too real, he had seen Gutierrez's son covered in blood and brain matter, screaming for his mother at the top of his lungs. Before that, he had heard the round as it whistled through the air... *shuuuuup*... and found its target in the boy's father.

Matt sat up, caught his breath, slowed his racing heartbeat.

Just a dream.

But so real.

The nightmares had been coming more and more frequently recently and with increasing intensity, which made him angry. He was a professional. In his time with the CIA, he had seen more than his fair share of death and destruction. Most often, he had been the cause of it. That his subconscious mind was now revolting against him was unacceptable. This was the job. The rules were simple: play well or get the fuck out of the game. Every operative seemed to know when their time was up. It showed itself in subtle ways, like thinking twice about an assignment, or, in this case, not pulling the trigger when ordered.

Perhaps this was where he was now.

Ferriman certainly saw it that way.

It was time to get out.

He had purchased the Soundview property as an investment during the economic crisis when the bottom had fallen out of the real estate market. At the time, every home on the street had been placed into foreclosure. He had bought all twelve of them. The investment company he had set up to complete the transaction was one of many he owned, all established using false IDs, and appeared to be completely legitimate. The Soundview properties had been acquired under the company *Eagle Investments*. Over the years, he had had the properties fixed up. All but three had been sold to new buyers. He'd kept this home for himself. The second property, which neighbored his own, he'd anonymously sold back to the original owners, an elderly couple whom he'd learned had lost everything in the crash, including their life savings, for the sum of one dollar. He also gifted them a check in the amount of one-hundred-thousand dollars to live out their golden years as they pleased. The third property was furnished and currently unoccupied.

Matt walked into the ensuite bathroom, stripped off his clothes, picked up the Sig Sauer P365 pistol, chambered a round, and stepped into the shower. He placed the weapon in the shower caddy between the shampoo and conditioner bottles where he could access it immediately if need be. The hot water cascading over his body from the rainfall shower-head helped to release the pent-up tension from his body. He took a deep breath, inhaled the rising steam infused with the calming scent of lavender and eucalyptus shampoo, and exhaled. He stayed under the water until it ran lukewarm, eyes closed, alone with his thoughts, then grabbed the weapon, stepped out, and toweled off.

He dried his hair, stepped into the walk-in closet, pushed aside the clothes hanging on the rack in front of him, and placed his hand on the biometric keypad integrated into the vertical safe mounted into the back wall. The door clicked open. He inspected the cache of weapons within it. The safe contained a Glock 19 9mm semi-automatic pistol with an extended capacity clip and ammunition, eight TNT core fragmentation grenades, a pair of EOTech ground panoramic night vision goggles, a Benelli M4 Super 90 gas-operated semi-automatic close range tactical shotgun, a MacMillan TAC-338 long distance sniper rifle, a M49 high-power spotting scope, military binoculars, Excalibur Micro 380 crossbow, and a Hammer Ocularis-fitted slingshot. The ammunition for all the weapons was housed in a separate drawer at the bottom of the safe. Satisfied all his gear and ordnance were accounted for, he closed and locked the safe.

The last few days on the road had been tiring. The longer Matt thought about it, the more he realized what he really wanted was to slip away, fall through the cracks, and know what it felt like to be anonymous.

The growl in his stomach reminded him he needed to eat. There was no food in the house. He would have to do a little grocery shopping later in the day.

Matt put on his bathrobe, walked to his front door, looked outside. The day was bright and beautiful. Perhaps a short walk would do him good. Besides, it had been a while since he had been in the neighborhood. From what he had seen of it when he'd pulled in last night the area had improved substantially over the years. But for all the progress that had taken place, certain pockets of Soundview still reflected the poverty of its past. Tenements and rent-controlled government high rises stood between re-gentri-fied million-dollar townhouse complexes. Soundview was going through a period of transition. While some families were thriving, it was plain to see that others were barely hanging on.

Matt dressed in the ballistic base layer compression vest, a pair of jeans, socks, a cotton T-shirt, his BulletBlocker jacket, and running shoes. He tucked the pistol into the small of his back, left his residence, and rounded the corner.

He had walked one block when a handwritten poster taped inside the window of a business across the street caught his eye. DISHWASHER NEEDED. INQUIRE WITHIN.

He thought about the job and what it could mean.

Anonymity.

Matt looked up, read the sign above the door: **Guiding Light Mission. Free Meals.**

He crossed the street and entered the premises.

Judging by the appearance of the patrons seated at the tables, the Guiding Light Mission provided meals for the homeless or underprivileged. Some individuals stayed to themselves, while others gathered in small groups and chatted while they ate their meals. The enticing breakfast smells of eggs, pancakes, toast, and coffee filled the room. The food smelled amazing. Matt's stomach growled.

"Welcome to Guiding Light," a voice called out. "Be with you in a sec. Have a seat. Make yourself comfortable."

Matt walked to a counter at the back of the mission from where he thought he'd heard the voice. "I'm not here for breakfast," he said. "I'm inquiring about the sign in the window. The dishwashing position."

An old man suddenly popped up from beneath the counter, startling Matt. His hands were full of tiny ketchup packets which he dumped unceremoniously on the Formica countertop. He bent over once more and retrieved an equal number of single-serve salt and pepper packets. Matt whipped his hand behind his back and instinctively clutched the handgrip of the pistol tucked into his waistband hidden beneath his jacket. When the man straightened up, he looked at him strangely. Matt released his grip on the weapon and rubbed his side as a distraction. He hoped the old man hadn't noticed the concealed weapon.

"You okay?" the man asked.

Matt nodded, came up with an excuse he hoped he would believe. "Back's a little stiff today."

The man laughed. "A young man like you with a stiff back? Try being my age and on your feet twelve hours a day. That'll give you a stiff back, a stiff neck... a stiff everything."

Matt smiled. "I'm sure it would."

The man extended his hand. "Name's Domenic Vitagliano. And you are?"

Matt shook his hand. He considered using one of his many aliases but gave his real name instead. "Matt."

"Ever work in a restaurant before, Matt?" Domenic asked as he unstacked several small plastic bowls and filled each one with ketchup packets.

"Every year as a kid," Matt lied. "Summer money."

Domenic nodded. "Huh," he said. "Where was that?"

"Upstate. Skaneateles. You know it?"

"By name, yeah. Never been there, though. What did you do?"

"Do?"

"At the restaurant. Wait tables? Greet guests?"

"Pretty much everything you can think of."

"Janitorial?"

Matt smiled. "Only if I couldn't get someone else to do it."

Domenic laughed. "You're preaching to the choir, brother."

"Is the position still available?" Matt asked.

"It is. But there's a catch to it you might not like."

"Oh?"

"We're a non-profit, so there's no pay. It's a volunteer position."

"I see."

"You looking to rack up some community service hours?"

"What do you mean?"

"Your PPO send you here?"

"PPO?"

"Probation and Parole Officer."

Matt shook his head. "I don't have a criminal record or a PPO."

"No problem if you did," Domenic said. "Everybody deserves a second chance to get straight."

Matt smiled. "Thank you, Mr. Vitagliano."

"Call me Domenic."

"Thank you, Domenic."

"So, what do you think?" Domenic asked. "If you're okay with the position being volunteer, we could really use the help. I'd love for you to join our little ragtag team of do-gooders. That is, if you still want the job."

"I do."

Domenic happily clapped his hands together. "Perfect. How soon can you start?"

"Right now, if that's okay with you."

"Conscientious. I like that. Say, you had breakfast yet?"

Matt shook his head.

"What's your pleasure?"

"That's okay, Domenic. I don't want to put you to any extra work on my behalf. You have guests to take care of. I'll grab a bite later."

"Nonsense," Domenic replied. "If you're going to be washing and drying dishes for the next few hours, you'll need your energy. How does pancakes, bacon, eggs, and coffee sound?"

"Like heaven."

Domenic laughed, pointed to the tables. "Coming right up. Have a seat. I'll bring it right out."

Matt smiled. "Thank you."

"My pleasure."

MATT ENJOYED a leisurely breakfast as he spoke with some of the mission's patrons, then took his place in the kitchen at the commercial washing and drying station. He enjoyed the simple manual labor for the next four hours. It felt good, as did the vibe of the mission itself.

In the small out of the way respite for the homeless, he had found what he was looking for.

He would stay in Soundview as long as he could. Deep down he knew the clock was ticking, that his past life as a CIA assassin was not one he could simply walk away from.

His days were numbered, and he knew it.

For now, he would accept the gift of internal peace the day had given him.

Then hope for one more.

6

Alpha Level 1

KYLA REESE'S STOMACH dropped the second she read the urgent encrypted message Langley had just sent her: IMMEDIATE ACTIVATION... PRIORITY TARGET... ALPHA LEVEL 1 C/K... DOSSIER ATTACHED. Matt Gamble's image stared back at her from the smartphone's screen.

Matt?

What the hell could he have possibly done to find himself the subject of an Alpha Level 1 Capture/Kill order?

She wanted to believe it wasn't possible, but she also knew the CIA didn't make mistakes. Her thumb hovered over the small red square in the lower right corner of the screen. She didn't want to press it, but knew she had no choice. They had sent the target package to her and no one else. She pressed her thumb against the screen and watched as the biometric authentication button turned from red to green, confirming to Langley that she had received the order and would immediately set out to find and eliminate the target. She had known Matt for years. They had worked together in the past. The first time was in Somalia, where they had been tasked with assassinating Abshir Omar, the leader of a group of well-organized and heavily funded modern-day pirates. Word had reached the Pentagon, and subsequently the CIA operations center in Virginia, that Omar was planning an assault on an American freighter scheduled to reach the Gulf of Aden in less than a week. What Omar did not know was that the cargo vessel *Borealis* was not a shipping freighter at all but an agency spy ship which had been dispatched to gather intelligence in the region. Combined Task Force 150 had been alerted to the chatter and placed on standby, but their services were ultimately not required. Working together, she and Matt had successfully infiltrated the pirate's compound one day before the planned attack, taken out Omar and his personal security team, and exfiltrated the country that night under cover of darkness.

Something had happened between them on that assignment. They had crossed the line, become intimate, which in their profession never turned out well. Immediately upon their return to the United States, each had received their new target packages. Kyla had been dispatched to Costa Rica, Matt to Saint Petersburg. They had lost touch after that, and it would have been a clear violation of agency protocol for them to have pursued an undisclosed relationship. To do so would be grounds for immediate dismissal. Kyla had spent the last three years doing her best to forget about Matt. She had fallen hard for him, and it took every ounce of discipline she had to put him out of her mind, which she had finally managed to do.

Until now.

She opened the file, read the details of his failed assignment which had prompted Langley to elevate the matter to Alpha-level status. Matt was to be handled with *extreme prejudice*. In other words, terminated. She committed the contents of the file to memory, then closed the phone and threw it across the room. It bounced off the couch pillows, fell to the floor. Not exactly the most respectful way to treat agency property. But at this moment, respect for the agency was the furthest thing from her mind.

She was furious.

They had tasked her with finding and killing the only man she had ever really loved, and the thought of having to do it was ripping her to pieces.

Perhaps there was something she could do. She could reach out to Langley, speak directly with Task Force Chief Cross, request to be assigned a different target package. But such an action would bring with it a litany of questions, none of which she was interested in answering. Inevitably, an internal investigation would follow. This would be done quietly, with neither of them knowing about it. But when Langley had completed their due diligence, they would come down on the two of them with everything they had. The details of their relationship would come out. Their lives would be dissected, their careers ruined. It was a no-win situation.

Kyla walked into the kitchen, picked up her personal cell phone from the counter, opened her contact list, selected Matt's name, stared at his number. It had been several years since they had spoken. They had discussed their relationship, even floated the idea of leaving the agency to pursue a life together. But once again professional responsibilities intervened, pulled them apart, and sent them to different regions of the world. Kyla recalled the pain in Matt's voice when he suggested it would probably be for the best if they both moved on, that as a couple they were simply not meant to be. She wanted to be with him more than anything else in the world and he with her. But the agency owned them. And now wheels had been set in motion. The mission was clear. Matt was to be put down.

Perhaps, she thought, being assigned Matt's Alpha Level 1 order was a blessing in disguise. If she could find him and talk to him there might be something she could do to set the matter straight. Best-case scenario, she could reach out to Langley and have the *kill* element of the order rescinded. She would insist he accompany her to the agency. Right now, she was the only operative in the agency who would be willing to spare his life on contact. He would have to listen to her. She would give him no choice. He had no other option.

Kyla took a deep breath, touched the screen, called his number.

Three melodic tones sounded, followed by a recorded message: "We're sorry, but the number you are trying to reach is not in service. Please hang up and try your call again. This is a recording."

Kyla ended the call. She gripped the phone tightly in her hand.

"Damn it, Matt," she said. "Where the hell are you?"

7

A Little To The Right

"LEAVE ME ALONE!"

The teenagers voice carried through the dining area of the Guiding Light Mission into the commercial kitchen where Matt was hard at work washing dishes. He heard the fear in her voice. With a quick spray, he rinsed the plate he had just washed, toweled it dry, then placed it atop the stack of clean plates on the stainless-steel counter. By the sound of it, a patron had crossed the line. It had been a busy lunch hour, the usual crowd, as he had come to learn. Good people mostly, some veterans of the street who leaned on the resources of the mission as a last resort, others victims of the times, having lost their jobs and homes through financial hardship. But for all who sought refuge, be it a warm meal or a roof for the night, the Guiding Light was there. The mission's policy was simple:

help anyone who needed it. There were only two rules of which they demanded absolute compliance from their guests. The first was that no alcohol, drugs, or weapons were to be brought onto the premises. The second, that bad behavior would not be tolerated.

Matt had been forewarned that disruptions occurred every once in a while. Domenic and his wife Carla referred to the offenders as one-timers; transient non-New Yorkers passing through the city on their way to god knows where.

Matt dried his hands, tossed the dishtowel onto the counter. He listened as Domenic and Carla spoke. Domenic chopped potatoes while his wife stood beside him, slicing carrots.

"I recognize their voices," Carla said. "They're back."

Domenic was angry. "I warned them before," he said. "I told them they are not welcome here. This is a place for those in need, not hoodlums."

Carla set down the knife. "You know who they are... *what* they are," she said. "These are not the kind of men who respond to warnings. You promised me if they returned you would call the police. Do that now, Domenic. Let them handle it."

"No," Domenic said. "I'm tired of this. I want them gone." He raised the knife. "If they won't pay attention to me, maybe they'll pay attention to this!"

Carla watched her husband storm out of the kitchen, butcher knife in hand. "No, Domenic," she pleaded. "Stop!"

Too late, Domenic walked out of the kitchen into the dining hall. Carla watched the door swing shut behind him.

Matt picked up the damp towel from the counter, slung it over his shoulder, grabbed a plastic bin used for collecting dirty dishes and tableware from the dining room, then followed the old man out of the kitchen, staying a few paces behind him, checking tables as he went, picking up used plates, glassware, and cutlery, and depositing them into the bin.

Francesca, Domenic's granddaughter, stood before the man who had grabbed her behind as she had walked past. She shoved him hard, forcing him to take a step back.

"Whoa," the man said with a laugh. "Bitch got some fire in her!"

The two men standing beside him chuckled.

He resumed his position in front of the teenager. "Come on, baby," he said. He held up the quarter-sized plastic baggy, flicked it with his finger. "You know what they say. Ain't no wham like Sapphire Slam."

"I know who you are," Francesca yelled. "Take your shit and get out of here!"

"Don't be like that, sugar," the man said. He moved closer, traced the packet down her cheek. "You too uptight, baby. Go on, take it. Body like that, first trip is on the house. You can pay me later."

Francesca slapped away the man's hand. "Go to hell," she said.

Domenic rushed to his granddaughter's defense, butcher knife at the ready, threatening the man. "Get away from her!" he yelled.

The man pushed Francesca aside. The teen fell to the floor. His hand instinctively went to the small of his back, beneath his jacket, wrapped around the handgrip of the gun concealed in his waistband. "Step off, old man," he warned.

Domenic raised the knife. "Or what?" he asked. "What are you gonna do?"

With the confrontation escalating rapidly, worried

diners grabbed their meager possessions, abandoned their tables, hurried away.

Matt set down the plastic bin, walked over to Francesca, helped her to her feet. "You okay, sweetheart?" he asked.

Francesca nodded. "I think so."

"Good," Matt replied. "Do me a favor. Your grandmother is preparing vegetables in the back. She could use some help. You mind?"

"But they're..."

Matt nodded. "I know. It's going to be all right. I'll take care of it."

"Grandpa!" Francesca pleaded.

"Your grandfather will be fine," Matt said. "Please, Francesca. The kitchen."

Francesca yelled at the drug dealer. "Fuck you!" she said, then turned on her heels and walked away.

When the young woman was out of earshot, Matt spoke calmly to Domenic. "May I have that?"

The surge of adrenaline coursing through Domenic's body from watching his granddaughter being assaulted fueled his rage. The blade shook in his hand.

Matt placed his hand gently on top of the old man's hand, slowly lowered his arm. "That's good," he said. "Easy does it, Domenic. Give me the knife. No one's going to get cut today."

The drug dealer smiled. "Yeah, old man," he said. "Give him the fucking knife before you hurt yourself."

With the insult, Matt felt Domenic's rage building once more. His hand re-tightened around the weapon's handle.

"Ignore him," Matt said. Before Domenic could react, he wrapped his fingers around the old man's wrist, pressed his thumb into the median nerve in his forearm, then squeezed gently. Domenic's hand opened involuntarily. The knife slipped out of his grasp. Matt took it and tossed the weapon into the plastic bin.

Domenic raised his finger, wagged it at the three men. "You're lucky I didn't kill you!" he said. "Leave here now! Take your filthy drugs with you and never come back!"

"Why would we do that?" the dealer replied. He raised the plastic packet, waved it at the crowd, called out. "You want money? You want off the street? Come over here. I got you."

Matt turned to the man. "Mr. Vitagliano asked you to leave," he said. "I think that would be a good idea."

The two enforcers took up positions around Matt. One moved beside him, the other behind.

Matt glanced over his shoulder, spoke to the man behind him. "Six o'clock."

The tough guy cocked his head. "What'd you say, asshole?"

"Where you're standing," Matt answered. "Six o'clock. If I were you, I'd move a little to the right. You're less of a target at five o'clock. But that's just my opinion." He turned, spoke to the man beside him. "You're perfect right where you are."

The drug dealer pulled his gun, jammed it in Matt's face. "Who the fuck do you think you are?" he asked. "Some kinda hero?"

Matt shook his head. "Not even close."

"No? Then what?"

Matt raised his arms, presented his empty hands. "I'm the guy you're gonna wish you'd never met."

With that, Matt grabbed the damp towel from his shoulder, wrapped it around the weapon, spun sharply, drove his heel deep into the man's groin, then pulled down hard on the towel. The dealer heard his arm break at the elbow as he fell to the floor. Gun now wrapped tightly in the towel, Matt swung the makeshift sling containing the heavy steel weapon against the temple of the man standing beside him, dropping him instantly. Facing his last would-be assailant, he snapped his foot into the man's groin, doubling him over, then wheeled around. The spinning back kick landed with devastating accuracy, whipping the man's head to the side. He crumpled to the ground at Matt's feet.

Matt stood over the three fallen men. "Get up," he said.

The men groaned, stirred.

"I said get up."

One by one, the men struggled to their feet.

"I'm never going to see you here again, am I?"

The men shook their heads.

"Good," Matt said. "Now leave before you piss me off."

8

Block B

MATT KEPT A close eye on the men as they left the mission. The leader of the group cradled his broken arm against his chest while barking orders at his underlings. One man held the door for him while the second followed behind. When the front door fell shut behind them, Matt handed the damp towel containing the gun to Domenic.

"Put this away," he said. "Keep it someplace safe. And don't take it out of the towel. You don't want your fingerprints on it."

Domenic took the weapon. He shook his head. "What you did. I've never seen anything like that before. You took out those men like it was nothing. How did you..."

"It's not important," Matt said. "All that matters is that Francesca and everyone else is safe."

"Thanks to you."

Matt ignored the compliment. "Those men. Who are they?"

"Street hoods," Domenic answered. "They work for a man by the name of David Forsythe. He's a real estate developer. Tries to come off as totally legitimate, but those of us close to the street know him better by his nickname, 'Diamond Dave.'"

"How original," Matt said. "What does it mean?"

"It's short for Diamondbacks, the name of his gang."

"A real estate developer *and* a gang leader? How does he pull that off?"

"Easily, I'm afraid." Domenic explained. "The gang came first. He formed the Diamondbacks when he was in high school. Before long, they had established themselves in the neighborhood as a pay-for-protection outfit. There wasn't a shopkeeper in the area who didn't hand over a tidy sum to them each month. If they didn't, they paid the price."

"Meaning?"

"Diamond Dave didn't give warnings. His men would enter their store just before closing or early in the morning. They'd move fast before the owner or their staff had time to react. They'd beat them up, break every display case in the place, steal their goods, then sell them on the street. Every once in a while, a store got lit up."

"They'd set it on fire?"

Domenic nodded. "It got to be the norm. Once every month, somebody's place would go up in flames."

"What did the cops do about it?"

"The police?" Domenic laughed. "You'd have better luck asking the Diamondbacks to just leave you alone. You've seen the neighborhood. This is a poor area. Which is why I set up the mission here. The people who live and work here are just getting by. They're easy targets for the gang. The problem is they're stuck between a rock and a hard place. They can't afford to pay for protection, and they can't afford not to."

"Then what do they do?"

"What every hardworking, non-violent, honest person tries to do," Domenic replied. "They work two, sometimes three jobs to keep a roof over their heads and food on the table. But it always ends the same way with the Diamondbacks taking everything they can from them. Last year alone, the number of suicides in our neighborhood jumped six hundred percent, from three to eighteen. There's no way to fight back. And it's getting worse. We have many low rent high-rise apartment buildings here. The Diamondbacks have started to expand their extortion business. Now they're going after the tenants in those buildings. We used to deliver bags of groceries to one family living there, Angelina Ruffalo, and her daughter Cassidy. Little girl's five-years-old and sweet as can be. Angelina uses a walker to get around. Car accident a few years back nearly killed them both. Lost her husband in the crash and left her with a bad hip. Block B was all they could afford, so they moved in. From what I've heard, it was a big step down. Angelina and her husband owned a successful house cleaning business. She can barely walk now because of the pain, so cleaning houses and most other jobs around here are out of the question. The woman's smart as a whip. She was studying graphic design at NYU before the accident but had to give it up. Couldn't afford the program anymore. Now, she and Cassidy get by on government assistance and with our help."

"You said you used to deliver groceries to her," Matt said. "Not anymore?"

Domenic shook his head. "We tried. Three times. It seems the Diamondbacks like the food we provide."

"What do you mean?"

"Our deliveryman refuses to go to the Block B apartments anymore. The first two times they stole the groceries. The third time, he tried to take them back. They beat him up. Broke two of his ribs. I feel terrible. I know how much Angelina and Cassidy need our help. But if we can't go to them and they can't come to us—"

"What do they need?" Matt interrupted.

"Excuse me?"

"Angelina and Cassidy. What groceries do they need?"

"Everything we can provide," Domenic replied. "Fresh vegetables, meats, dairy."

"Put an order together."

Domenic stared at his new friend. "Are you sure about this?"

Matt nodded. "Like you said, they can't come to you, and they need your help. I'll take care of it."

"Before you go any further with this Matt, you'd better think it through," Domenic urged. "The Diamondbacks won't take kindly to seeing an unfamiliar face in the complex, much less one who won't do what they tell him to do."

Matt shrugged. "Maybe for me they'll make an exception."

Domenic shook his head. "I doubt it."

"I'd prefer to try the diplomatic approach first."

Domenic crossed his arms. "And if that doesn't work?"

Matt picked up the bin of dirty dishes, headed for the kitchen. "Then they'll have a problem."

9

Born To Do This

TASK FORCE CHIEF Cameron Cross entered Ferriman's office. "Where are we with Reaper?" he barked, demanding to know the current status on the search for the rogue assassin.

The director stood. "I've assigned an operative to track him down."

"Who?"

"Kyla Reese."

"Why her?"

"They have a history. Gamble trusts her."

"I don't give a damn about trust," Cross blurted out. "What sort of history?"

Ferriman cleared his throat. The TFC was a difficult man to deal with at the best of times. The standing joke in the department was how perfectly his surname suited him.

Today, the matter with Matt had him worked up more than usual. "They've worked together in the past, pulled each other's asses out of the fire on more than one occasion," he replied.

"You think she can bring him in?"

"I'll give her seventy-two hours. If she hasn't rectified the situation by then, I'll assign another operative."

"Why so long?"

"Gamble is in the wind. We can't locate him."

"Isn't that why we have fucking drones?"

"Yes, sir. It is."

Cross was expecting a better answer. He shook his head, opened his hands. "*And?*"

"We've been tracking the GPS on his vehicle since he left his position."

"Then what are you waiting for? Intercept him and take him down."

"We can't, sir."

"Why not?"

"Because we have a signal, but no vehicle."

"That doesn't make any sense."

"I'm afraid it does."

"How's that?"

"Tech suspects it's a ghost signal."

"Meaning?"

"That somehow Reaper has manipulated his vehicle's GPS to show it's in motion when it's not."

"How could he do that?"

"They figure he hacked the Navigator's software and programmed it to follow a ghost route away from his actual position."

"Can't we track the signal back to its source?"

"That depends. If it's coming from an actual computer, yes. If it's emanating from the dark web, the signal could be pinballing off dozens of servers all around the world every few seconds. We'd never find it."

Cross shook his head. "Fucking computers."

"Yes, sir."

"The operative you've assigned, Reese. You're confident she can get the job done?"

"I am."

"She better, or it'll be your ass on the line."

"Understood, sir."

"Keep me posted on this matter twenty-four seven. Got it?"

"Yes, sir."

"Good. Now go get me Gamble."

Cross stormed out of the room.

Ferriman waited until Cross had left his office, then walked to his window and stared outside. "Jesus, Matt," he said aloud. "Why didn't you just take the fucking shot?"

He hoped he'd made the right choice in assigning Kyla Reese to find Matt and either bring him in or take him out. He'd perused her file before arriving at his decision. Besides Matt, he would have been hard pressed to find an operative better suited to the task. Reese's reputation as a strategic thinker and skilled assassin set her apart from her colleagues. If anyone could get inside Matt's head and talk him down it was her.

Ferriman walked to his desk, opened Matt's file. His steel-blue eyes stared back from the page. He was six-foot two, powerfully built, cut, athletic. The personnel file provided insight into his past. Connie and Stephen Gamble, his parents, were deceased. Both had been adrenaline junkies. His passing came as the result of a shark attack while SCUBA diving off Australia's Great Barrier Reef. Hers occurred ten months later when her parachute failed to open during a recreational jump. Although the chute was found to have been properly packed, it was speculated that Connie, who had been having an impossibly difficult time coming to terms with her husband's horrific death, had tampered with it and committed suicide. The claim was never proven. In the same year that Matt lost his parents, he found the strength to complete his final year at Baylor University, graduating with degrees in both Political Science and Public Policy and Administration.

He had come to the agency's attention several months after graduating while teaching an evening self-defense class at Baylor. Holding dual black belts in both Brazilian Jiu Jitsu and Krav Maga, Matt had been covertly put to the test. Unbeknownst to him, one student in his class was not actually a student at the university but a deep cover CIA operative. One night after class, she confided in Matt that she had been receiving strange phone calls at all hours of the night and that she suspected she was being stalked. Matt offered to accompany her on her walk home to her apart-ment, which was located a short distance from the campus. Just before reaching the building, two men appeared from the shadows and tried to force the woman into a van parked at the side of road. Matt immediately put his skills to use. He laid out the men, breaking the jaw of the first and four ribs of the second before they dove into the van and make good their escape. Two days later, Matt was approached by the woman and her handler, a representative of the Department of Defense. They revealed the truth behind the attack. It had been a set-up, a test to see if he could handle himself as advertised. He had passed with flying colors. They extended an offer to him to work for his government. It was the right time in his life. His parents were gone, and he had no one else to care for except Charlie the Tuna, who was actually a goldfish. Matt accepted, found a good home for Charlie, and soon found himself a trainee at Camp Perry in Williamsburg, Virginia, the military base which housed 'The Farm,' the CIA's covert training facility. There he was educated in the use of a variety of weapons and explosive ordnance, learned how to parachute, SCUBA dive, rappel, handle a boat and car using high speed evade and escape maneuvers and, most importantly, how to survive being tortured should he ever be captured by the enemy. The training had been grueling, but Matt had left an indelible mark on his instructors. His proficiency in all areas far exceeded those of his fellow recruits.

Ferriman read the note which his training officer had written in his file. The statement was simple but powerful: 'Candidate Matt Gamble is one of the finest recruits ever to complete this program. In short, he was born to do this. I hereby recommend him for immediate posting to the field.'

The director closed the file, tossed it on his desk.

He was born to do this...

Matt was capable of taking out anyone who came after him.

He hoped Kyla Reese could find him.

He also hoped that when she did, he wouldn't kill her.

10

Hold Out

"OF COURSE, SIR," the receptionist said. She returned the telephone handset to its cradle, stood, then addressed the three men seated in the posh lobby of Forsythe Group, LLC. "Mr. Forsythe will see you now," she said. "Please follow me."

The men had never before been to the building. To receive an invitation to meet with David Forsythe in person was almost unheard of. It was well known that his most trusted and highly regarded associates, those who comprised his inner circle, could be counted on one hand. The men glanced about nervously as they accompanied the pretty receptionist down the long corridor. One side of the hallway featured a glass walled meeting room. Inside, a group of men and women stood around a large architectural model on a long table in the center of the room. They were deep in conversation and appeared to be arguing over the models features. A member of the group walked to a whiteboard at the end of the room and began making notes. Below the seventeenth-floor meeting room lay New York's Central Park.

When they reached the end of the hallway, the receptionist knocked lightly on the door.

"Enter."

"Mr. Forsythe," she said, "Mr. Edwards, Mr. Glenn, and Mr. Evans to see you."

Forsythe smiled. "Thank you, Gretchen," he said. "Gentlemen, please come in."

Gretchen held open the door for her boss's guests, then quietly closed it behind them.

The real estate developer's office was sparsely appointed. His desk was one-of-a-kind, a boxed frame design consisting of steel construction beams painted bright red and set under a thick glass desktop. The bespoke piece had been custom made for him by one of New York's preeminent industrial design artists. On the desk sat a telephone, blotter, Mac computer, mouse, and lamp. The mirrored, backlit bookshelf that ran the length of one wall deceived the eye and gave the room the illusion of being twice its actual size. Elegant glass sculptures and framed photographs adorned its shelves. On the credenza behind Forsythe, a silver serving tray presented a selection of rare Scotch whiskies and Baccarat crystal tumblers. Three luxurious armchairs sat in front of his desk.

He remained seated, motioned to the chairs. "Take a seat," he said.

"Thank you," the men said. The two waited until the man with the broken arm had seated himself, then took their place in the remaining chairs. Forsythe noted the man's plaster cast resting in the black cloth sling, said nothing. He leaned back in his chair, propped his elbows on the armrests, steepled his fingers, and stared silently at the men. Broken Arm looked down, adjusted his sling. The man to his left cleared his throat. The other shifted uncomfortably in his chair.

Forsythe stared at the men, then addressed the man in the sling. "Am I to understand the old man did this?"

Broken Arm spoke first. "Sir, I can explain."

"Shut up, Darnell," Forsythe said. He sat forward, pointed his finger at the men seated on either side of him. "Is this what I get for giving you your own crew? Glenn with a broken cheekbone, Evans with a fractured eye socket, and you with your arm snapped at the joint. Are you kidding me?"

Darnell Edwards tried to speak in his own defense. "He took us by surprise."

"The old man?"

Darnell shook his head. "It wasn't Vitagliano."

"Then who are you talking about?"

"Some guy. A dishwasher."

"A *dishwasher* did this... to all three of you?"

The man with the fractured eye socket who had taken the full impact of the towel-wrapped semi-automatic spoke next. "He was working in the back," he said. "I saw him come out of the kitchen."

The recipient of the spinning back kick and bearer of the broken cheek bone spoke next. "Yeah," he said. "I think he was a dishwasher, maybe a cook. He followed behind the old man, picking up dirty dishes. He stepped in after the old man pulled a knife on Darnell."

Forsythe was fuming. He stared at Darnell. "You let the old man get the drop on you?"

Darnell shook his head. "He came out of the kitchen with it in his hand. Looked like he was ready to use it just 'cause I pushed his bitch to the floor."

"What *bitch?*"

Darnell shrugged. "Dunno. Niece, granddaughter maybe. Whatever. Chick was smokin' hot. Didn't like that I grabbed her ass. Big effen deal."

"And that led to this?" Forsythe asked.

"No, man."

"No, *what?*"

Darnell blushed. "I apologize, Mr. Forsythe. No, *sir.* Things went to shit when Vitagliano's guy got all up in my face and forced me to pull out my piece. Before we knew it, all three of us were on the ground and my fucking arm was busted. Doc says it'll be eight weeks before it heals."

"I don't care if it takes eight goddamn years," Forsythe said. "Your arm is the least of my concerns. I have investors ready to move on that property and Vitagliano is the last holdout. I need that mission gone. The three of you had your marching orders and you fucked up... royally."

"Give us a chance to make it right, Mr. Forsythe," Spinning Back Kick said. "We can take him out."

Forsythe folded his arms. "Forgive me if I don't share your level of confidence, seeing as how well that worked out for you the first time you tried."

Fractured Eye Socket spoke next. "It will be different this time, sir. We weren't ready for him then. We are now. He won't even see it coming."

Forsythe stood, walked to his bar, opened the bottle of Glenmorangie 1971, poured himself a drink, sipped the

Scotch, set down the tumbler on the credenza. "All right," he said. "One last chance. Get it done."

"Yes, sir," the men replied.

"Don't make me regret this," he said. He turned his back to the men, stared out the window, looked down over Central Park. "Now get out of my sight."

11

Touch And Go

MATT OPENED THE front doors promptly at seven o'clock and welcomed the morning patrons into the mission. The old building had never been retrofitted to accommodate individuals with disabilities. To make up for this, Francesca, Domenic, and Carla always took a few minutes out of their busy morning to assist their mobility challenged customers into the mission and help them to a table. When the crowd had been welcomed, the family returned to the kitchen and began serving food to their guests. While Domenic worked the grill, Carla plated the morning breakfast of two eggs, pancakes, two slices of bacon, and buttered toast. Francesca served from behind the counter. Matt assisted the infirm by carrying their tray to their table and bringing them a cup of steaming hot coffee.

Several patrons stared at Matt and spoke in hushed tones as he went about his duties, wiping down tables, collecting dirty plates, cups, saucers, tableware, and returning them to the kitchen. Francesca had been called to the tables on more than one occasion. Matt felt their eyes on him. He tried to put their inquisitive glances out of his mind and cursed himself for not having listened to his inner voice. He should have left well enough alone, turned his back on the incident, stayed in the kitchen, minded his own business. The execution of his new plan had called for him to remain anonymous, to stay in the shadows and off the radar. He wanted to forget the Agency and his association with it as he passed through this town and moved on to the next. But most of all, he wanted to forget who he was and all he had done.

Francesca stopped him as he passed her on the way to the kitchen. "Got a second?" she asked.

Matt set down the heavy plastic tub. "Sure."

The teen fidgeted uncomfortably as she spoke. "About what happened yesterday…"

Matt said nothing, waited for her to find the words.

"Thank you."

Matt picked up the bin. "Don't mention it."

"No, really," Francesca said. "If you weren't here and did what you did, my grandfather would be in the hospital right now, or worse, not here at all."

Matt knew what she was referring to. He shook his head. "They would have roughed him up, but I don't think they would have killed him."

"What makes you so sure?"

Matt shrugged. "I'm not."

"The way you handled them. You made it look easy, practiced."

"I got lucky."

Francesca crossed her arms. "I don't think so."

Matt glanced at the dishes in the bin, nodded towards the kitchen. "These aren't going to wash themselves. You mind?"

Francesca stepped aside, allowed him to pass.

Matt glanced back at her as he walked away. "I'm glad you're okay, Francesca," he said.

WHEN MATT HAD FINISHED DRYING the dishes, he tossed the damp towel aside, retrieved a fresh one from the rack above the rinsing station, wandered into the food storage area, and found Domenic sitting in his chair behind the tiny desk he called his office, hands folded in his lap. He looked worried, preoccupied.

"Everything all right, Domenic?" he asked.

Domenic shook his head. "Do you remember the young woman I told you about yesterday?"

"Angelina Ruffalo?"

"That's right." Domenic sighed. "She admitted her daughter to the hospital last night."

"Cassidy? What happened?"

"The Diamondbacks happened."

"What do you mean?"

Domenic fisted his hands, shook them. "I wish I was eighteen again," he began. "I was a Golden Gloves boxer back in my day. Almost made the Italian Olympic team. If I could, I'd go down to Block B right now and clean house. I'd beat the living hell out of every one of those sons of bitches."

"Relax, Domenic," Matt said. "Tell me what happened to Cassidy."

Domenic settled down. "Angelina had no food in the house, and Block B is not the place where you knock on your neighbor's door to ask for help, so she left the apartment with Cassidy. I was told they were coming here when it happened."

"When what happened?"

"Two of the Diamondbacks grabbed Cassidy and pulled her away from her mother," Domenic explained. "From what I was told, they taunted her. Poor thing was diagnosed with a brain injury due to a car accident. Everyone knows she finds it difficult to keep her balance. The child can't walk anywhere without her canes. Old Tom and his wife, the couple you helped seat this morning, witnessed it all. Bastards kicked her canes out from under her. After she fell, they stood her up, waited for her to fall again, then kept doing it, again and again, until finally she struck her head on the pavement and passed out. Angelina was powerless to stop them. Someone managed to flag down a cop car, which in this neighborhood is a rare sight. They drove her to Montefiore Medical Center in Westchester. She's been in the ICU all night."

"What's her condition?"

Domenic took a deep breath, let it out. His voice cracked when he spoke. "I don't know."

"Can you find out what room she's in?"

"Why?"

"I'd like to visit with her and her mother."

"But they don't know you."

"All the better."

"I'll come with you."

"No."

"Why not?"

"You don't want any part of this, Domenic. You have this mission and a restaurant to run. That's enough."

"What are you going to do?"

Matt stared at Domenic through cold eyes. "I'm going to meet the neighbors," he replied.

12

Tick-Tock

KYLA REESE GRABBED her go bag and headed out the door. She did not know where to find Matt, but the simple act of being in motion made her feel like she was taking some kind of action. Langley would want an update as soon as possible. They had given her seventy-two hours to find him. After that, all bets were off, and the game would change. As good as Matt might be on his own, he wouldn't stand a chance against a team of highly trained CIA assassins.

When she reached her car, she opened her phone and reviewed the target package information once more. The agency's predictive analysis software had identified three key areas where Matt was most likely to go if faced with a worst-case scenario such as this. The first was New York

City. His cellular tracking history indicated he had visited the city frequently over the years. The second was Los Angeles. The third Toronto.

Los Angeles was out. Kyla knew him well enough to know that he would never remain in California after failing to execute the target in Big Sur. He would want to put as much distance between himself and the state as possible.

Toronto, Canada, was a possibility. He had mentioned before how much he loved the city and the country. But that would mean attempting to cross the border from the USA into Canada. Even if he disguised his appearance and presented the Canadian border authorities with an expertly designed fake passport, it wouldn't be a risk he would be willing to take.

That left New York City.

With a population of nearly nineteen million people, it would be an easy place to hide, at least for a while. But not forever.

Matt was up against the CIA itself. He had to know his days were numbered.

Kyla started her car and headed for the airport. When she arrived in New York City, she would contact the agency and request the location of the closest safe house and armory. They would outfit her with all the weaponry and tactical gear she would need to bring Matt in.

She hoped it wouldn't come down to that.

She suspected she knew where he might be hiding out. He had mentioned it years ago during their assignment in Somalia while they were in bed together. He had called it his favorite place in the world: Soundview, in The Bronx.

Kyla reached LAX, booked a flight to New York City.

"Be there, Matt," she said to herself as she took her seat and waited for the aircraft to taxi to its takeoff position on the runway. "For your sake, please be there."

13

Commotion

MATT HEARD THE commotion at the serving counter. Domenic was angry, yelling. He left the dishwashing station to find out what was wrong.

Domenic stood at the counter shaking the sheet of paper the man had just handed him.

"I'm sorry, Mr. Vitagliano," the man said. "They're called flash inspections for a reason. You're not supposed to know when they're coming."

Domenic threw the paper into the air. The man watched it flutter to the ground.

"This is ridiculous!" Domenic objected. "By-law inspectors were in here last week. They examined the place thoroughly. Now you're telling me I'm due for another inspection? This will be the third this month! Stop wasting my time and my tax dollars!"

"I understand how much of an inconvenience this must be for you," the man said. "Every inspection is different. Your last two inspections were for rodent control and kitchen hygiene. This is for gas and mechanical. We'll need to shut you down for the evening in order for us to complete our work. It's a safety issue."

"The whole evening?" Domenic yelled. "We can't do that! We have people staying here for the night. They have nowhere else to go. What am I supposed to do, turn them out into the street? That's precisely what they came here to avoid!"

The city inspector had been patient to this point, but his tolerance with Domenic was wearing thin. He spoke firmly, decisively. "I get that. I don't want to see these people displaced any more than you do. But rules are rules, and you're no more above them than anyone else. You have one hour to get everyone out of the building. It will take our people approximately three hours to complete the inspection. We'll notify you once the work is complete. You can re-open then or in the morning. There'll be a green sticker on the door if the premises has passed inspection. If it hasn't, the door will be padlocked until we have completed the required mechanical or gas line upgrades. Again, Mr. Vitagliano, I apologize. The more cooperative you are with us now, the quicker we can be done with this."

"Ridiculous," Domenic repeated.

"One hour," the city worker said. "Have a good evening, sir." He turned and left the mission.

Matt had been standing quietly behind Domenic, listening to the conversation. When the man left, he walked up to the counter and stood beside him. "Everything okay, Domenic?" he asked.

Domenic shook his head. "Same nonsense, different day. It's getting so that a business owner can't turn around in this city without being inspected for this or fined for that. These inspections have gotten out of hand. I have to deal with it here and at the restaurant. Some days I wonder if it's even worth the frustration anymore."

"I can appreciate how you must feel," Matt said. "If it's any consolation to hear, there were sixty or more people in here today who would be in worse shape if it wasn't for you, Carla, and Francesca and your decision to keep this place open."

"Thank you, Matt. I appreciate that."

Matt placed his hand on Domenic's shoulder. "It's just for one evening. I'm sure your patrons will understand. Are there other missions in the area you can refer them to?"

Domenic nodded. "Yes, there are."

"Call them," Matt said. "Tell them what's happening and ask if you can send your people to them for the night. I'm sure they'll be willing to help."

"All right," Domenic agreed. "I'll do that now."

"Good. I'll make the rounds, let everyone know what the situation is, and help them pack up. Try not to worry. Everything will be back to normal by tomorrow evening. You'll see."

"I hope so."

"It will be," Matt said. "Go on. Make your calls. I'll get started."

·   ·   ·

AN HOUR LATER, Matt joined Domenic, Carla, and Francesca outside the Guiding Light Mission. When the last of their guests had left the premises, Domenic closed and locked the door. "I hate the idea of having to give them a key," he said. "Damn city regulations."

"Is that required?" Matt asked. "I could stay here, let them in, then lock up behind them when they leave."

Domenic nodded. "The letter stated it was necessary. They give themselves a wide inspection window. Anytime between now until five o'clock in the morning."

"I guess they figure doing the work at night is less impactful to the business than closing you down during the day."

"Which, for most businesses, it would be."

"Why not take advantage of it?" Matt suggested. "Make it a family evening."

Carla slipped her arm around her husband's waist. "That's a brilliant suggestion, Matt," she said. She pulled him closer and smiled. "Come on, Dom. I'll make you your favorite dinner."

Domenic smiled. "Veal parmigiana with spaghetti and meatballs?"

"Exactly."

Domenic laughed. He turned to Matt, winked. "Now you know why I'm fat."

Matt smiled. "I wouldn't call you fat."

"No? What would you call me?"

Matt hesitated. "Content."

Carla laughed, patted Domenic's stomach. "He's carrying an extra twenty pounds of *content*," she said. "But that's just the way I like him."

"You'd better," Domenic replied. "Those extra twenty pounds are your fault."

"*My* fault?"

"For being such an excellent cook."

Carla laughed. She turned to Matt. "We live just a few blocks away, Matt," she said. "Would you care to join us for dinner?"

Matt smiled. "Thank you for the invitation, Carla," he replied. "I've already made plans for the evening. Another time perhaps?"

Carla nodded. "Of course. You're welcome at our home any time."

"I appreciate that."

"Where are you off to now?" Domenic asked.

"Montefiore Medical Center," Matt replied. "I'd like to check in on Cassidy Ruffalo, make sure she's okay."

"It's good of you to do that, especially since you don't even know the family."

"After what you told me about what happened to her, I haven't been able to get her off my mind. That isn't right. She needs to know someone is looking out for her now."

"Like I said, Matt. This is not a safe neighborhood. And those men are dangerous. You'd better watch your back."

"I will."

"Are you sure I can't convince you to join us?" Carla pressed.

Matt smiled. "I'm sure."

"All right," Carla replied. "Have a good night, Matt."

"I will." Matt winked at Francesca. "Take care of your grandparents on the walk home, okay?"

Francesca smiled. "Always."

Matt watched the family walk away, turned up the collar

on his jacket, pulled his baseball cap down over his eyes, then headed up the street in the opposite direction. He thought about what Domenic had told him about the Ruffalo's, how both mother and daughter had been taunted, the crippled girl assaulted, and the head trauma she had received as a result of the heinous and unconscionable act that had been perpetrated against her. It made him angry.

He kept his head down, picked up his pace.

Eight blocks to go.

14

Gentry Fine Cigars

DAVID FORSYTHE FELT his cell phone vibrate, removed it from his jacket pocket, checked the display. The caller ID read **GENTRY FINE CIGARS**. He took the call. "Hello?"

"Good evening, Mr. Forsythe," the caller said. "This is Martine calling from Gentry Fine Cigars. How are you this evening?"

"I'm well, Martine," Forsythe replied. "And you?"

"Very good, sir."

"How can I help you?"

"You placed an order with us three days ago."

"Yes."

"For two boxes of the Fuentes Crisco Cohiba's. Is that correct?"

"It is."

"We now have them in stock, sir."

"Excellent."

"Would you like us to deliver them to the address you provided?"

"Yes, please."

"Of course, sir. We're running a little late with our deliveries today. I hope that won't be too much of an inconvenience."

"How late is late?"

"Would 1:00 A.M. be all right?"

"That should be fine."

"Very good, sir. If it's all the same to you, I'd like to take care of our brokerage fee now."

"Bitcoin?"

"Yes, sir."

"Send me the encryption key. I'll remit payment right away."

"That would be appreciated."

"Of course."

"Just to confirm, you'd like one box delivered to the first floor, the other to the second."

"That's correct."

"Wonderful. I'll see that our courier follows your instructions to the letter."

"Thank you."

"Will there be anything else, sir?"

"No, thank you. That should suffice for the time being."

"Excellent. I'm sure you'll find the brand to your liking. They're worth every penny."

"I'm sure they are."

Forsythe opened his computer, navigated to the Gentry Fine Cigar company website, clicked the My Account tab, opened his private inbox, found the message containing the encryption key, tapped the link, reviewed the amount due and payable... $50,000.00... sent the payment. "Done," he said.

Martine received confirmation that the transaction had been successfully completed.

"You're all set, Mr. Forsythe," he said. "Payment has been received and your delivery scheduled."

"Thank you, Martine."

"Have a pleasant evening, sir."

"You as well."

Forsythe ended the call.

This was not the first time he had done business with Gentry, and it wouldn't be the last. Even though he had never met anyone from the company in person and did not know where in the world they were located, they had always been reliable.

He checked his watch. It was early in the evening. By the time the packages were delivered, he would be in bed.

He closed his computer, slipped it into his shoulder bag, called for his driver, then left the office for home. He would sleep well tonight.

Gentry had everything under control.

15

The Girl In 302

MATT ARRIVED AT Montefiore Medical Center in Westchester, waited for the lobby receptionist to finish typing on her computer keyboard. Finally, she looked up. "May I help you, sir?" she asked.

"Cassidy Ruffalo," Matt said. "What room is she in?"

The receptionist entered Cassidy's name into the computer. "302," she replied.

"Thank you."

Matt rode the elevator to the third floor, walked to the central station, inquired with the duty nurse. "Cassidy Ruffalo?"

The nurse nodded. "Follow the red line on the floor to the end of the corridor. Her room is on the left. 302."

Matt walked down the corridor, found the room,

71

stopped just outside the door, listened, waited. Inside, he heard a woman talking through her tears. Angelina Ruffalo, Matt thought. Cassidy's mother.

"Is she going to be okay, Doctor?" the woman asked. "Please tell me she's going to be okay."

The doctor's response was neutral, his delivery practiced. "We're doing the best we can, Mrs. Ruffalo," he replied.

"Has there been *any* improvement?" Angelina asked.

"Very little, I'm afraid. In Cassidy's case of intracerebral hematoma, the blood in her brain has changed, which presents a problem. What was a solid clot has now become liquid. I made a small hole in her skull to suction out the blood. That seems to be working. She's experiencing less swelling now than she was when she was first admitted, but she's not out of the woods yet. Her recovery will take time. This type of cranial trauma is unpredictable. All we can do is treat the symptoms as they present." The doctor paused. "I'm sorry, Mrs. Ruffalo. I wish I could offer you more positive news, but I'm afraid I can't."

Angelina sniffled. "I understand. Thank you."

"Of course."

Matt waited for Cassidy's surgeon to leave the room. He debated whether to introduce himself to the woman. He had heard the fear and sheer exhaustion in her voice. She was emotionally drained, deeply vulnerable. No, this was not the time. Right now, what she needed more than anything else was privacy and time alone with her daughter. Perhaps he would return tomorrow, check in on them again. With any luck, the night would bring an improvement in Cassidy's condition. The thought of the family's plight made Matt's blood boil. They had done no wrong. The girl was an innocent victim and far too young to be forced to endure such a life-threatening ordeal. Regardless of his own situation, he could not - would not - let this go.

Something had to be done about the Diamondbacks.

Matt returned to the central station, spoke to a young woman. The uniform she wore suggested she was a nursing student. "Excuse me," he said. "Do you have a pen and a sheet of paper I can use?"

The teenager smiled. "Of course," she replied. She searched the desk, handed Matt the items.

"Thanks," Matt said. He wrote a few words on the page, folded it, handed back the pen. "Can you do me a small favor?" he asked.

The young woman looked up. "If I can."

Matt smiled. "My sister is with my niece in 302. I told her I'd come by to visit with them, but I can't stay. Would you mind giving her this note?"

"Certainly," the teen said. "I'll be happy to."

"Thank you."

Matt left the central station, walked to the end of the corridor, watched as the young nurse entered Cassidy's room, then turned the corner and headed for the elevator. As he rode the car to the ground floor, he recalled the painful but honest words the doctor had said to Cassidy's mother. *"Intracerebral hematoma... she's not out of the woods yet... her recovery will take time."*

The elevator doors opened. Matt stepped into the corridor, exited the hospital. He needed to clear his mind. The long walk back to his townhouse would do him good, help to burn off his pent-up anger. After that, the heavy bag hanging in his basement would be getting one hell of a workout.

As Matt rounded the corner, he saw a commotion in the distance.

An elderly man and his wife were being accosted by a young street punk.

His thoughts turned back to the struggling family and the doctor's last words... *if she ever fully recovers.*

No more, he thought. This ends now.

Matt stepped up his pace.

The kid couldn't have picked a worse night.

16

Guest Pass

THE BONDI HOTEL in The Bronx was anything but luxurious, but that didn't matter to Kyla Reese. She had stayed in worse places. A three out of five-star property at best, its location was the reason she'd chosen the Bondi. It was nearest to the address of the Bronx CIA operations safe house she had been given. Upon her arrival at LaGuardia Airport she had contacted the house, requested a guest pass, and received a confirmation code via text. She was expected.

After dropping her overnight bag in her room, Kyla walked to the address of the inconspicuous brownstone. She climbed the stairs, pressed the intercom button, looked up. A camera, housed above her in a plastic bubble, whirred as its lens narrowed and focused. Kyla waited for it to complete its facial identity scan. The door's unlock buzzer sounded. Kyla pushed it open, stepped into the vestibule, closed the door behind her.

A young man stood waiting for her; a pistol fitted with a sound suppressor pressed against his leg.

Kyla glanced at the weapon, then at the man. "You must be the welcoming committee," she said.

The man motioned with the weapon. "Against the wall. Raise your arms."

Kyla placed her hands against the wall.

"Step back. Spread your legs."

Kyla complied. She glanced over her shoulder as the station agent smoothed his hands up and down her neck, chest, back, and legs as he patted her down. "Most guys buy me dinner before I let them go there," she said.

"Gee," the agent replied. "I've never heard that one before."

"Was it as good for you as it was for me?"

"Spare me the one-liners, Reese. You know the protocol as well as I do."

Kyla dropped her arms, turned around, faced him.

"What do you need?" the agent asked.

"What have you got?"

"Everything."

Kyla winked. "You're making me weak in the knees."

"You always such a smartass?"

"As a rule, yes."

"Seriously. Your requirements."

"Personal carry, plus something light, foldable, and easily concealed with serious stopping power."

The man nodded, entered his security passcode into a touch panel located beside a heavy steel door situated beside them. The door clicked open. "Not a problem," he said. "Come with me."

Kyla followed the agent into the safe house. "You got a name?" she asked.

"Yes."

"Funny."

"Tanner."

"Good to meet you, Tanner."

"Uh huh." Tanner ignored the pleasantries. "This your first time here?"

Kyla nodded. "Yeah."

The interior appointment of the safe house looked normal. Its living room featured a wall-mounted flatscreen television, a couch with end tables, two reclining chairs, a wall mirror, and a bookcase. Off the main floor hallway was an ensuite bathroom and large kitchen. Next to the kitchen, a split staircase led up to a second floor and down to the basement.

"Nice, isn't it?" the agent said.

Kyla nodded. "Not bad."

"Beats agency safe houses from the old days."

"Old days?"

"Single room, bare concrete walls, a ceiling light, and a chair."

"Nice to see we're in Uncle Sam's good books."

The agent smiled. "It might look all bright and shiny but trust me. This place is a fucking fortress. Want the nickel tour?"

"Sure."

"There's a Keurig in the kitchen. I was about to make myself a coffee. You want one?"

"Sounds good."

Tanner entered the kitchen, opened a cupboard door. "We've got light roast, dark roast, and hazelnut. Help yourself."

Kyla selected a dark roast pod from the container, slipped it into the holder, pressed down the lever, waited for the machine to brew the blend. Seconds later, she was sipping the hot coffee.

Tanner brewed a fresh cup of light roast for himself, added a touch of milk. "Come on," he said. "Let's get you kitted up."

Kyla followed the station agent downstairs. At the foot of the stairs, a heavy steel door guarded access to the room. Tanner punched in his access code. The door unlocked. He smiled as he pushed the door open. "Welcome to the candy store."

Motion sensors turned on the lights as they entered the room. Harsh white light from the overhead florescent fixtures illuminated the armory.

Kyla whistled. "Wow," she said. "Candy store is right."

The walls of the room were filled with an assortment of handguns, tactical rifles, knives, and scopes.

Tanner spoke. "Like I said, I've got everything you'll need, including explosive ordnance."

"I prefer to travel light," Kyla replied.

"No problem. Help yourself."

Kyla selected a Heckler and Koch MK23 pistol and a KAC MK23 sound suppressor from the wall. Tanner handed her a loaded magazine. Kyla slipped it into the weapon, locked it in place. She raised the pistol, pointed it at the wall, tested its weight.

"Good?" Tanner asked.

Kyla nodded. "I'll also need a shoulder harness with dual clip holders."

"Coming right up." Tanner opened a drawer, removed the item, handed it to the operative.

Kyla removed her jacket, slipped into the leather harness, fitted the weapon into its holster. Tanner loaded two additional magazines, handed them to her. She inserted them into the rig, pointed to the wall. "I'll take the ARES FMG as well."

Tanner removed the folding submachine gun from the wall, handed it to her. "Clips full," he said. "She's ready to rock and roll. You planning to take on a small army or something?"

Kyla thought of Matt. "Let's hope it doesn't come to that."

"Anything else?" Tanner asked.

Kyla shook her head. "I'm good."

Tanner raised his coffee mug. "If that's the case, happy hunting."

Kyla clinked her mug against Tanner's, thought about what he had just said. Would it come to that? Once she found Matt - if in fact she could - would he listen to her and come in quietly like she hoped? Or would she be forced to take part in a hunt she wanted no part of?

She needed to start searching for him as soon as possible. In less than seventy-two hours, Director Ferriman would open the order. Blood would be in the water, and the sharks would start to circle. After that there would be no turning back. Matt would be a dead man walking.

Kyla slipped the subcompact ARES FMG submachine gun into her purse and the MK23 into the small of her back. She covered the weapon with her jacket. "Thanks, Tanner," she said.

Tanner nodded. "Anytime."

They left the armory, climbed the stairs.

Tanner opened the door for Kyla. "Stay safe, Reese," he said as she stepped outside. "If you need any more party favors, you know where to find them."

Kyla nodded. "Copy that."

17

Give Me A Name

THE ELDERLY WOMAN held on to her purse strap for dear life. "No!" she said. "You can't have it! Go away! Leave us alone!"

Her husband stepped forward, grabbed the punk's hand, tried to wrench it free of the strap. The man's attempt to defend his wife was met by a powerful blow to the side of his face. The assault dropped him. He fell to his knees, cried out in pain. "My knees!" he screamed. "God, my knees!"

"That's what you get, asshole!" the punk said. He lifted his shirt, pulled out a handgun, pressed its muzzle against the back of the man's head. "You wanna meet Jesus tonight, grandpa? Come at me one more time. Go on! Do it!"

The old man raised his hands, pleaded. "We don't want any trouble."

"Goddamn right you don't," the punk yelled. "I'll splatter

your senior citizen brains all over the fucking sidewalk. You feel me?"

The elderly woman began to cry. "It's only money, Charles," she said.

"I don't care, Beatrice," Charles said. "He's not having it." Charles fought against the pain in his arthritic knees, tried to pull himself to his feet. The punk pressed the muzzle even harder against his skull, prevented him from rising.

"Look at me, you old gray-haired fuck," the punk said.

Charles looked up.

The punk turned the weapon on Beatrice, pointed it at her face. "Your old lady has five seconds to give up the purse or you go home a widower. Five..."

Tears fell from Charles's eyes, rolled down his face. "No, Bea."

"Four..."

"I'm sorry, Charles. I have to."

"Three..."

"It's all we have, Bea. You can't."

"Two..."

Beatrice closed her eyes.

"One," the punk said. "Night, bitch!"

The punk felt his feet leave the ground as Matt surprised him from behind, lifted his gun hand high into the air, swept his feet out from under him, brought him down hard onto the sidewalk. The punk's head struck the cement with a sickening crack.

Matt turned to the couple. "You two okay?" he asked.

Beatrice helped her husband to his feet. The bewildered seniors stared at the stranger.

"I... I think so," Charles replied. "You, Bea?"

Lost for words, Beatrice just nodded.

"Good," Matt said. He looked down at the punk. The kid couldn't have been any more than sixteen years old. Having been rendered senseless by the severe takedown, he moaned, then slowly came around. He looked up at Matt, tried to struggle. Matt grabbed his wrist, locked it, applied pressure.

The kid screamed. "Jesus, man! You're breaking my fucking wrist!"

"That's the general idea," Matt said.

"Fuck you!"

Matt bent the punk's wrist back even more, listened as he cried out. "You owe this nice couple an apology," he said.

"Let go!"

"You want *me* to start counting down?" Matt asked. "Because if I do, I can absolutely guarantee it won't end well for you."

"Okay! Okay!"

"Okay... *what?*"

"I apologize!"

"Say it like you mean it. And not to me, to them."

The kid relented. "I'm sorry I tried to steal your purse."

Matt turned to the couple. "Sounds like he means it. What do you think?" Matt increased the pressure once again. The kid screamed out in agony. "Christ, it hurts!" he yelled. *"Stop, stop, stop, STOP!"*

"That's enough," Beatrice said. "Don't hurt him anymore. Let him go."

Charles's opinion differed from his wife's. "The hell he has," he said. He stepped forward, then kicked the punk between his legs as hard as he could.

Matt released his hold on the kid's wrist after watching

him receive the excruciating blow. The punk rolled onto his side, drew his knees to his chest, cried out.

"*Now* he's had enough," Charles said.

Matt leaned over, slapped the kid's face, drew his attention away from the pain coursing through his genitals. "Look at me," he said.

The punk tried to look up, couldn't.

"You want more?"

The kid shook his head.

"Empty your pockets."

The kid opened his tear-filled eyes, looked up. "What?"

"You heard me. Empty your pockets or I'll do it for you."

The kid turned his head away. "Help yourself."

Matt rifled through the punk's pockets, first his pants, then his jacket. He tossed the contents on the ground beside him, inventoried the score. Nearly one thousand dollars in cash, plus a zip-sealed plastic bag filled with dozens of tiny, heat-sealed plastic bags. Matt examined the quarter-sized bags. Each contained a small amount of blue crystals. He recognized the baggy from his previous run-in with the thugs at the Guiding Light Mission.

He shoved the packet of drugs in the kid's face. "Who gave you this?" he asked.

The punk looked at the baggie, then turned away. "You don't want to mess with that, man," he said.

"Answer the question."

The pain from the old man's blow was beginning to abate. The kid's cocky attitude returned. "Brother," he said, "you must have a death wish."

"Give me a name."

"No thanks. I value my life... such as it is."

"Do you value your ability to use your right hand?" Matt

asked. He grabbed the kid's wrist once more, applied pressure, bent it back.

The kid screamed. "*Fuck!*"

"That's an expression, not a name."

"Diamond Dave!"

"You mean David Forsythe?"

"Yes! Jesus, let go of my fucking wrist!"

Matt released his hold on the teen. He picked up the cash, handed it to the elderly couple. "Take this," he said. "It's yours now."

Charles shook his head. "We know where that money came from," he said. "We want nothing to do with it."

Matt nodded. "I understand."

The punk looked up, smirked. "Good fucking answer, old man. You pocket that money or my baggies and you're as good as dead."

"I don't think so," Matt said. He took the cash, folded it, shoved the wad into his pocket, stood, picked up the gun and baggies full of drugs, walked to a nearby gutter, threw them into the sewer drain, watched as the darkness swallowed them.

The kid yelled out. "Are you fucking crazy? That was three grand worth of Slam! You know what's gonna happen to you now? You're a fucking dead man!"

Matt ignored the threat, returned to the elderly couple. "Will you two be okay to walk home?"

Charles stared down at the teenage delinquent lying at Matt's feet. "We should be."

Matt saw the fear in his eyes. "You worried about him?"

Beatrice nodded. "A little."

"Don't be. He won't be bothering anyone for a while.

Besides, he'll be spending the rest of the night in Emergency."

The kid looked up. "What the fuck are you talking ab—?"

Matt leaned over, grabbed his wrist, twisted it hard and fast.

Snap.

The punk let out a horrific howl. He grabbed his broken wrist, pulled it to his chest, rolled on the ground.

Matt stood, turned to the old couple. "What do you say we call you a cab?"

Charles and Beatrice stared at the kid, then back at Matt, nodded. "Thank you," Charles said.

"My pleasure," Matt replied.

18

Out Of Nowhere

A NGELINA RUFFALO STAYED with her ailing daughter fifteen minutes past the posted patient visiting hours. The nursing staff had given the woman extra time to collect herself after she had broken down upon reading the note the nursing student had given her. She grabbed the bed rail for support, stood, leaned over Cassidy, kissed her gently on her forehead. "I'll be back in the morning," she said. "Sleep well, baby. Momma loves you."

She rolled her walker in front of her, locked the hand-brakes, then lifted herself up. Once she was confident that she had achieved her balance, she released the brakes. Using the walker for support, she exited Cassidy's room, took the elevator down to the first floor, exited the hospital, and hailed a cab. The driver helped her into the back seat of his car, then folded her walker and placed it in the trunk.

The driver glanced in his rearview mirror. "Where to?" he asked.

"Soundview, please," Angelina replied. "The Block B apartments."

The driver nodded. "You've got it."

Angelina said little on the drive back to her apartment building. She spent the commute in quiet contemplation, wondering how her life had come to this. It had once been so good, so full. As a family, they were happy, their future promising.

The car crash three years ago ended that.

Cassidy was two years old. Miguel, Angelina's late husband, had buckled his infant daughter securely into her car seat before they'd left their Long Island home to drive into Manhattan to enjoy Sunday dinner with his parents. The route was familiar, one they had taken dozens of times in the past. Angelina recalled their moods that evening. Miguel was feeling on top of the world and shared the reason for his happiness with his wife. He had met with the president of a large commercial real estate company earlier in the day and been awarded the cleaning contracts for all four of his downtown office buildings. The deal would generate a second revenue stream in addition to that of their residential customer base and put their steadily growing cleaning business solidly in the black. They had worked hard at growing the company over the last year. Miguel had taken a chance, reached out to the mogul. With the financial support of his father, he had hired six new staff members to help them take their business to the next level. It had been a gamble, a roll of the dice, but Miguel was confident he could secure enough new contracts to keep their new staff members steadily employed. He had big dreams for the business and was not afraid of working as many hours as needed to make it a success.

The Mercedes had come out of nowhere. At the moment of the car accident, they were stopped at a red light, waiting for it to change. Miguel had turned in his seat to play tickle-toes with Cassidy. Angelina had lowered her visor mirror to touch up her makeup. Neither of them had seen the Mercedes cross over the meridian, hurtle toward them, and slam head-on into their car. On impact, Angelina's world went black. Two hours later, she awoke in the E.R. and received the horrific news. Miguel was gone. He had been killed on impact. Cassidy had suffered a traumatic brain injury. She had been left with a broken leg and severe damage to both hips. Following her husband's funeral, she was forced to face the reality of her situation. With her mobility severely impaired and now unable to work, she made the calls she dreaded. She reached out to the accounts Miguel had worked so hard to secure and informed them that the business had been forced to close. Miguel had maintained a minimal life insurance policy. After paying his funeral expenses and the exorbitant hospital and out-patient physical rehabilitation costs for both her and her daughter, they had been left with very little money to live on.

News of a vacancy in the Block B apartments had come to her through a former employee. The six hundred square foot unit was a far cry from the elegant brownstone she was accustomed to living in, but it was affordable. She and Cassidy needed little more. They would turn it into a home. They had no other choice.

When the driver arrived at Block B, he exited the vehicle, opened the trunk, removed Angelina's walker, opened it, and rolled it around to the rear passenger door. He opened the door, took Angelina's hand, helped her out of the vehicle.

Angelina grabbed the walker's handgrips, steadied herself, smiled at the driver. "Thank you," she said.

"My pleasure. You need help? I'm fine with leaving the car here for a few minutes if you need assistance getting into the building."

"That's very kind of you, but no," Angelina replied. "I can manage from here."

"You sure?"

"Yes." She opened her purse, paid the fare. "Thank you for the ride and the offer to help."

"No worries." The driver glanced at the two men standing in the lobby of the run-down apartment building. "You know those guys?" he asked.

Angelina looked up, shook her head.

The driver persisted. "You sure you don't want me to walk you inside?"

She smiled. "I'll be okay."

"All right. But if it's all the same to you, I'm going to wait here for a minute, keep an eye on you until I see you enter the elevator."

"You don't have to do that."

"I know, but I'm going to anyway. Have yourself a nice evening."

"Thank you," Angelina said. "You as well."

. . .

ANGELINA RODE the elevator to the seventh floor, entered her sparsely appointed apartment, closed and triple-locked the door behind her, hung her jacket in the hall closet, kicked off her shoes, then rolled across the living room to her couch where she sat down, then removed the note from her purse and read it again: STAY STRONG. YOU HAVE A FRIEND. EVERYTHING WILL BE ALL RIGHT.

A friend was something she had not had for a very long time.

She folded the note, placed it on the table beside her, stretched out on the couch, lay on her pillow, covered herself with a blanket, thought about Cassidy, and said a prayer.

Exhausted, she fell into a deep sleep where her subconscious mind conjured up nightmares of the accident accompanied by the terrified screams of bystanders.

19

Cohiba Behike

THE LANEWAY BEHIND the Guiding Light Mission provided the perfect cover for his assignment. Two sodium-vapor streetlamps, each at opposite ends of the service road, cast the laneway in a jaundice yellow light. The mission, which was in the middle of a strip of twelve commercial properties, received no light. Its rear entrance door was steeped in shadow, as too was the fire escape ladder attached to the wall which led up to the roof.

The man scouted the alley, found a discarded wooden shipping pallet, angled it against the wall beneath the metal ladder, slipped his foot between the slats, tested its stability. The heavy pallet held his weight. Using it for support, he jumped up, grabbed the lowest rung of the metal ladder, pulled himself up, then climbed the structure. When he had reached the top he stepped onto the roof, dropped low, and surveilled the surrounding area. At this early hour of the morning no lights were on in the apartments across the street. Even the usual sounds of the city seemed quieter, as if this section of The Bronx had decided a night of rest and relaxation was in order.

Confident he had not been seen he hurried to the skylight, removed a flashlight from his belt, turned it on, inspected the inner perimeter of its housing, looked for indications that it was wired to a security system, found none. He switched off the light, slipped it into his pocket, removed and unzipped his backpack, withdrew a pair of bolt cutters, dispatched the single padlock which served as the skylights only protection against intruders, and lifted the bubble. From the backpack he removed a climbing rope knotted every six inches, tied one end to the fire escape ladder, then returned to the skylight, dropped the rope into the darkness, slipped the two cigar boxes inside his jacket, then lowered himself down. He remained motionless at the bottom of the rope for a moment, listening to the sounds of the building, heard none. The evacuated mission was quiet.

Satisfied he was alone, he dropped to the floor, removed one of the two cigar boxes he had assembled per the requirements of the assignment, then walked the second floor until he found the perfect location for it in a bookcase. He opened the box, set its timer to fifteen minutes, placed the firebomb between two books on the bottom shelf, then proceeded downstairs to the first floor. He ran through the dining hall into the kitchen, found the supply closet, activated the timer, placed the second firebomb between two gallon-sized containers of cooking oil, then rushed back to the second floor and exfiltrated the premises the same way he had entered it. He climbed the rope, hoisted himself up and over the rim of the skylight, untied the rope from the ladder, coiled it quickly, then descended the ladder. When he had reached the ground he shoved the rope into his backpack, then walked calmly to a waiting van.

The driver waited until the man had climbed in, then put the vehicle in gear and slowly drove away. "Any problems?" he asked.

The man shook his head. "None. Beaumont did his job well."

"Anyone can pass for a city inspector these days," the driver said. "People are so fucking stupid. Show up with a clipboard and an official-looking letter, give them a convincing story, and you're good to go. How long until the fireworks?"

"Ten minutes."

"You set both devices?"

"That was the contract, wasn't it?"

The driver looked at his passenger. "You know the rules. I have to ask before letting the company know that the job is on schedule."

"Yes."

"Good." The driver raised his hand, motioned to the glove box. "Boss sent you a present. Check it out."

The bomber opened the glove compartment, removed a cigar box, opened it, smiled. "Nice," he said.

"Damn right, baby. Those are Cohiba Behike's. They're four hundred bucks a pop."

The bomber closed the box, checked his watch. Five minutes to go.

"You want me to call the boss?" the driver asked.

The bomber nodded.

The driver placed the call, provided the required update.

"Circle the block," the bomber said. "Park down the street."

"That's not a good idea."

"Just do it."

"It's not protocol."

"Fuck protocol. I want to see the show."

The driver shook his head as he turned the corner. "You're pushing your luck, which means you're pushing *our* luck."

"Don't be such a puss."

"Beats the shit out of getting caught."

"What are you talking about? The cops have no reason to stop us."

"No? How about being in the vicinity of an explosion at one-thirty in the morning?"

The bomber conceded. "All right. Park one street over. I want to hear it when it goes off."

The driver circled the block, found a suitable street, parked the van. "How much longer?"

The bomber checked his watch. "Two minutes."

The driver smiled. "Don't ya just love blowing up shit for a living?"

The bomber removed a cigar from the box, lit it, puffed away on the expensive tobacco, nodded. "There's no better feeling in the world."

One minute to go.

20

Jab, Strike, Kick

MATT PULLED THE street punk to his feet, sent him on his way, then waited for a cab to arrive. He helped the elderly couple into the back seat, confirmed that they were indeed okay following their traumatic run-in with the drug-peddling street hood, pre-paid their fare home, and cautioned them they would be wise to avoid the area for a while. It was clear to him now that Forsythe was attempting to lay claim not just to his neighborhood but possibly all of Soundview.

Arriving home, Matt lay on his couch, tried to sleep, couldn't. Behind closed eyes, his mind was fully awake. Random scenes played in his imagination... *Domenic threatening the Diamondback enforcers with the butcher knife and the actions he had taken to subdue them... witnessing the actions of the street kid as he threatened to murder the elderly couple if they failed to comply with his demands... the face of the target whom he had been tasked with eliminating but refused to kill in the presence of his young son... the knowing that he had now made himself a priority one agency target and that at this very moment every attempt was being made to hunt him down.*

Matt sat up, buried his face in his hands, tried to quell the onslaught of the visions in his head, couldn't. He tried to distract himself by turning on the television and watching the news, but to no avail. When frustration finally overtook preoccupation, he walked into the kitchen, removed a bottle of water from the refrigerator, and downed the cold liquid at once. He collapsed the plastic bottle, tossed it into the recycle bin beneath the sink, then headed downstairs to the basement.

Matt had finished the room to suit his needs. Behind the drywall, he had cladded the walls with 65 STC-rated mineral wool insulation which rendered it virtually sound-proof. A long metal track ran lengthwise along the ceiling and terminated at the far end of the basement. From it hung a paper target imprinted with a bullseye. He would periodically use the indoor shooting range to help him work out his frustrations, but tonight required more strenuous activity. A heavy bag hung in the corner next to a home gym. Matt walked to the bag, slipped on his training gloves, began punching and kicking it, lightly at first, focusing more on form than power as he warmed up. The thoughts that had kept him from sleep soon returned. Before long, more powerful and brutal blows followed each practice jab, strike, and kick. Fifteen minutes later, now drenched with sweat, Matt stopped. He pushed the heavy bag away from him, let it swing back and forth. The workout had helped. He had tired himself out. All that remained was the need for a long, hot shower, followed by a restful night's sleep. He removed the training gloves, tossed them on the floor, headed upstairs to take a shower.

The hot water felt good on his body. He stood under the rainfall shower head, closed his eyes, focused on the sound of the falling water, calmed his mind. Tomorrow, when he had finished his day washing dishes at the mission, he would begin a deep dive into the life of David Forsythe and the Diamondbacks, then formulate a plan to take back the neighborhood, assuming he would be able to remain in Soundview a few more days. He had covered his tracks as best he could when he had left California, but he was also well aware of the agency's reach. He knew in his gut he could not stay off their radar forever. He would have to act fast.

Matt stepped out of the shower, dried off. He felt relaxed. A good night's sleep was in order.

He had just drifted off when he was awakened by the sounds of police, fire, and ambulance sirens speeding past his bedroom window. Matt climbed out of bed, parted the drapes, searched the street for the reason for the emergency response.

Around the block, just a short walk from his townhouse, Matt observed a sea of flashing red, white, and blue lights dancing off the walls of the neighboring buildings and high rises.

A chill ran down his spine.

The Guiding Light Mission was on that block.

Matt dressed quickly, opened his nightstand, grabbed

his Sig handgun, shoved it into the small of his back, slipped on his jacket, shoes, and baseball cap, then headed out the door.

He had a bad feeling about this.

A very bad feeling.

21

An Excellent Job

ONE STREET OVER the explosion was so loud and so powerful that the two men seated in the van felt the vehicle shudder. The bomber opened his door, stepped outside, crossed in front of the van.

The driver lowered his window, spoke to him. "Where do you think you're going?"

"Wait here," he replied. "I'll be back."

"I parked here so you could *hear* the explosion," the driver replied. "You said nothing about going to the building."

"Are you forgetting who's in charge?"

The driver paused. "No."

"Then shut up."

The driver shook his head. "This is a stupid idea, man. You're gonna get us both caught."

The bomber flipped him the finger. "My operation, my rules," he replied.

He crossed the street and walked down the sidewalk towards the intersection. Beyond the row of walk-up town-houses, he watched as fingers of orange flame licked skyward from the roof of the mission. It was a beautiful sight.

Slowly, the doors of the neighboring townhouses began to open. Homeowners, concerned for the security of their property and their relative proximity to the explosion, exited their homes and took to the street. Some ran past the bomber to the corner, while others ventured into the middle of the road to glimpse the action. The bomber drew his collar tight around his neck, pulled his baseball cap down over his forehead. By the time he had reached the intersection, a sizable crowd had gathered across the street from the row of businesses of which the Guiding Light Mission was one. While police set up emergency barricades and kept onlookers a safe distance away from the raging inferno, fire personnel tended to their rigs. The bomber too kept his distance, stayed at the back of the gathering crowd, watched the scene as it unfolded. Across the street, the mission's front windows blew out of their frames from the intense heat of the white-hot blaze. Screams erupted from the crowd as glass rained down on them, forcing them to cover their face and eyes. Concerned for their safety, the fire captain instructed the police to order them further back from the scene. A second fire vehicle soon arrived. As the driver eased the rig into position, fire personnel exited the vehicle and executed their roles. While some attended to storage compartments and the pump panel, others deployed water hoses. The ladder began its angled ascent above the building. One firefighter grabbed a fire hose, climbed the ladder, opened the nozzle. A powerful cone of water streamed forth and blanketed the roof of the mission and its neighboring businesses. Above the roar of the water and the organized chaos on the ground, the fire captain could be heard issuing commands to his team through the ladder engine's loud-speaker. A second explosion soon followed the first.

The bomber smiled. He knew where it had come from. The commercial kitchen.

The contract had gone off without a hitch. The Guiding Light Mission was no more.

A young man stood beside him. He held his father's hand as he watched the building burn. "Dad?" he said.

The father looked down at his son. "Yes, Eric?"

The boy's voice shook. "You think anyone was inside the building when it blew up?"

His father shrugged. "That's possible, son."

"If they were, they'd be dead, right?"

The father nodded. "I can't see anyone surviving a fire that bad."

"Me neither."

While some members of the battalion moved inside the mission, other firefighters took up positions atop the build-ing. The bomber watched as they cut holes in the roof to vent the smoke and fire while their colleague's made entry from below. There was nothing more that could be done to save the mission. The fire had reduced it to an incinerated shell. Attention had now shifted from firefighting to fire prevention in an effort to minimize the risk to the adjoining businesses. He removed his smartphone from his belt, snapped a few pictures of the smoldering structure, viewed them, felt pleased with himself. He had done a superb job. The photos would make excellent additions to his collection.

The boy again. He pointed to the paramedics standing beside their ambulance. "How come they're not going in?" he asked his father.

"They'll only respond if they're needed."

"Shouldn't they at least ask if they can help?"

His father shook his head. "They'll need to have permission from the fire captain before they'll be permitted to enter the building. It's not safe for them to do so yet."

The boy's voice cracked. He was getting upset. "But there could be people inside who need them!"

"Come, Eric," his father said. "You don't need to see any more of this. It will give you nightmares."

"But Dad..."

"No buts, son. Let's go."

The bomber turned away as father and son walked past him. He watched them return to their townhouse a few doors down. He waited for the front door to close behind them, then crossed the road and returned to the van.

"Well?" the driver asked the bomber as he opened the door and slipped into the passenger seat.

"It couldn't have gone any better."

The driver smiled. "I guess that's why they pay you the big bucks."

"It is."

The driver pulled the van away from the curb, proceeded slowly up the street. "Martine will be pleased," he said. "So will his client."

The bomber nodded. "They'd better be."

22

Bump-and-Lift

MATT FELT HIS stomach drop as he rounded the corner and observed the members of the fire platoon exiting the charred remains of the Guiding Light Mission. The intense heat of the raging inferno had decimated both the first and second floors of the facility. The windows were gone. The acrid smell of scorched metal hung heavily in the air. News crews that had arrived too late to the scene hurried to set up their equipment. A throng of reporters, microphones in hand, rushed past Matt, cornered the fire captain, began peppering him with a barrage of questions. How had the fire started? Had anyone perished in the blaze? Was arson suspected? Not wanting to be captured on camera, Matt fell back into the pressing crowd and listened as the captain responded to their questions. No, thankfully, no one had died in the fire.

At this moment, arson was not being considered as the cause of the blaze but was yet to be ruled out by the Bureau of Fire Investigation. Yes, the proprietors of the mission had been contacted and were on their way to the scene. No, there had been no significant damage to any of the adjoining units, all of which were vacant. Although they were able to work fast and contain the blaze, they could not save the mission.

Outside the police barricade, three people fought their way past the reporters until they reached the fire captain.

Domenic, Carla, and Francesca had arrived.

Matt kept his distance and his head low, wary of the many smartphone cameras surrounding him as curious onlookers busily photographed, recorded, and live-streamed the scene and the couple's reactions to their discussion with the fire chief. He tried to overhear the conversation but couldn't. Matt wanted to go to the family, to reach out and comfort them, but he knew that was not possible. At this very moment, the event was being shared and broadcast across numerous news agencies and social media platforms. Broadcasting his face on the news or online could expose him to the agency, and the consequences of their learning of his current location could prove deadly.

While conducting covert operations overseas, Matt had become familiar with the extent of the damage and destruction a well-placed firebomb could create. Most obvious was the smell. The incendiary device - or devices - which had taken out both floors of the mission, had employed a specialized gel-fuel mixture which included magnesium, napalm, aluminum, and white phosphorus. Judging by the appearance of the now gutted mission, the fire had been instantaneous. It had sucked all available oxygen out of the building at the time of the detonation. The ingredients used to make this device had been formulated to pull air upward and initiate a catastrophic firestorm within the building. The air currents which had entered the building from the street when the windows blew out served to fuel the fire and accelerated the destruction.

There was no doubt in Matt's mind that this fire was no accident.

This was the work of a professional arsonist.

Domenic was right. He and his family were being targeted. In the short time since he had returned to Soundview, he had learned enough about the neighborhood to suspect who was behind the attack: David Forsythe and his gang, the Diamondbacks.

Matt slowly distanced himself from the crowd, took cover behind a delivery van parked across the street. He surveyed the onlookers, studied their body language. One individual immediately caught his attention. The kid was in his mid-teens. Unlike the others, he was not on his phone filming the action, which suggested to Matt he was more fascinated with watching the blaze and observing its chaotic aftermath than anything else. After a minute, he stepped away from the crowd and began to walk in Matt's direction. Matt waited until he was close by, then knelt and fiddled with his shoelaces. As the kid walked past he fell in step behind him, watched him as he pulled his cell phone out of his back pocket and placed a call. Matt listened to the one-sided conversation.

"It's Benny. Yeah, it's done. Man, your boy knows his stuff! It was crazy. The place burned to the ground. The old man? Yeah, he's here. Nah, he won't be a problem anymore.

You need me to hang around? Okay, I'm here if you need me. Thank you, sir. Goodnight."

The kid ended the call, shoved the phone into his back pocket.

Matt approached him quickly from behind as they reached the intersection. Ahead, the light was red. The kid waited to cross the street.

Matt bumped into him hard, slipped his hand into his back pocket.

The kid whirled around, challenged Matt. "Yo, what's your problem, man?"

Matt apologized. "Sorry," he said. "I wasn't watching where I was going. Are you okay?"

"Am I *okay?* Of course I'm okay! Do I look like a fucking invalid to you?"

"Not at all."

The kid slipped his hand into his pocket, produced a butterfly knife, flicked it open, threatened Matt with the weapon. "Get your ass away from me before I fuck you up!"

Matt stepped back. "It was an accident. Again, I apologize."

The kid put away the knife. "Find someplace else to cross the street."

"Sure thing. No problem."

The light turned green. Matt waited until the kid was halfway across the intersection, then turned and headed back in the direction he had come. He slipped his hand into his jacket pocket, retrieved the kid's phone which he had stolen from him during the tactical bump-and-lift. He pressed the Home button, tried to open it. Locked.

No matter. He had the necessary software back at his townhouse to hack into the device and download its call, text, and search history. But there was only one thing he was interested in at this moment. The identity of the person the kid had been talking to.

Matt pocketed the phone, glanced over his shoulder. The kid was now long gone and apparently none the wiser for the theft of his phone. He knew exactly what he looked like. If he needed to find him again, he would.

When he reached the site of the burned-out mission, Matt stepped behind a delivery van and watched as the fire crew folded their hoses and returned their equipment to their trucks.

Domenic sat on the curb in front of the mission which had once been his pride and joy, his head buried in his hands. Carla sat on his left, Francesca his right. His wife and granddaughter held him.

Matt could hear the old man sobbing.

He crossed the street.

23

An Unsettling Feeling

THE BEDROOM WINDOW of the Bondi Hotel might just as well have been made of paper rather than glass. Kyla lay in bed listening to every sound the street offered from below her third-floor room. Garbage containers being rolled down driveways and placed in front of homes and businesses to be emptied in the morning. The bouncing of a basketball in a nearby community court. The hooting and hollering of young men as they played the game with no consideration for those trying to sleep. The barking of a dog. The voices of a group of boisterous teens as they passed beneath her window. Try as she might, she could not settle her mind. Her thoughts returned to Matt and the capture/kill order. Every minute not spent searching for him was another closer to his being taken out by the members of the kill team Ferriman would dispatch if her mission proved unsuccessful. She couldn't allow that to happen. However severe the situation was that had brought Matt to this junction, it couldn't possibly be bad enough to warrant the agency taking his life. She had to find him first, put an end to the search, and save his life. She only hoped he would let her help him.

Kyla leaned over, flipped on the table lamp beside her, stared up at the ceiling. There was no point in trying to sleep any longer. She needed to get up, move, exercise, wear herself out. Perhaps then sleep would come more easily.

She stood, looked out the window, glanced up the road. The emergency vehicles she had heard whose loud sirens had roused her from a light sleep had stopped, but the distant reflection of their dancing service lights lit up the far end of the street. Whatever the emergency was it had been serious to warrant a major response. With the prospect of sleep now totally off the table she walked to her closet, dressed, slipped the Heckler and Koch pistol into the small of her back and the sound suppressor into her pocket, put on her jacket and shoes, and left the hotel room. The young couple who entered the elevator when she reached the second floor smiled at her. Kyla acknowledged them while giving them the once over. Years of training had taught her to never take a situation for granted, no matter how obvious or innocuous it might appear to be. She glanced at their clothing, looked for signs of a concealed weapon, saw none. Unless their intention was to resort to the wet work of a knife, they appeared to pose no threat. Regardless, she moved to the back of the elevator, positioned herself into the corner of the lift, slipped her hand behind her back, cradled the handgrip of her gun until they reached the ground floor lobby, then waited a few seconds for the couple to exit the elevator ahead of her before she stepped out. This was for her protection. Had she misread the couple and they were, in fact, foreign assets who had been dispatched to find and kill her, she would still have time to duck behind the elevator's closing doors, hit the call button for the top floor, use the doors as cover against gunfire as they closed, then ride the car up to a point of egress faster than the couple could race up the adjoining stairwell. This wouldn't have been the first time she had found herself in such a situation. Five years ago, in Cape Town, such an incident had occurred. She had taken a flesh wound to the thigh in the ambush. The bullet had missed its mark and only grazed her, but it had been too close a call for comfort. Her attackers had not been so lucky. She had drawn her weapon and gotten off two quick shots. Both had found their mark. The male operative dropped instantly, his female partner a second later. He had taken Kyla's round to his chest. As the elevator doors closed, Kyla had watched the gun fall from his hand, his body drop to its knees, then fall face first down onto the granite lobby floor, very dead. Judging by the way the woman had fallen, with no bodily response of any kind, the bullet had forged a violent path through her brain and ricocheted around in her skull, rendering her incapable of retaliation. Since that night, Kyla never again let her guard down in public, not even for a second. Throughout her career, she had been personally responsible for taking out terrorists, dictators, despots, and various enemies of the state. She suspected her identity was on the blacklist of many covert organizations. Sometimes the secret world of espionage was not so secret after all. Just as her government surveilled foreign powers and sanctioned the elimination of its assets, so too did they. Key

American operatives, of which Kyla was one, constantly faced the threat of assassination.

Satisfied the couple posed no danger, Kyla raised her hand, broke the sensor beam of the closing elevator doors, waited for them to open, then stepped into the lobby. She waited for the couple to leave the hotel through the front doors before following them outside.

A familiar smell caught her attention as she walked up the street towards the emergency vehicles which had now turned off their lights. A fire truck drove past her while a second remained at the scene. The emergency was over. Kyla's curiosity got the better of her. She walked towards the corner. The closer she got, the smell in the air became stronger. An unsettling feeling washed over her. She recognized the smell. Napalm. No, she thought. She had to be wrong. There would be no reason to deploy an incendiary military chemical on the streets of sleepy little Soundview. But past experience informed the present. She had smelled the invisible weapon many times after she had deployed it on foreign soil. There was no mistaking it. Kyla's body tensed. Her situational awareness rose to high alert. Could this have anything to do with Matt? If so, why?

She approached the intersection with caution. Across the road, firefighters hosed down both the decimated structure and its adjoining units. A group of teens had gathered. Kyla joined them.

"You guys know what happened?" she asked.

"No idea," one of them answered. "But look at the damage! I've never seen anything like it. I'm surprised it's still stand—"

Before the young man could finish speaking, the roof of the fire ravaged building suddenly collapsed.

Across the street, Kyla watched a man act quickly as the building fell, hurrying an elderly couple and a teenager away from the danger to the safety of the fire truck. Even in the smokey darkness, she recognized him immediately.

It was Matt.

The teens had seen enough, moved on.

Alone on the corner, Kyla calculated her next move.

24

"You'll Need Proof."

DOMENIC STARED AT the smoldering remains of what had been the Guiding Light Mission. He wanted to speak but couldn't find the words.

Carla held his hand. "It will be okay, Domenic," she said. "We have money set aside. Between that and the payout from the insurance company we'll be able to start over. And when we do, we'll make the Mission bigger and better than it was before."

"I don't care about bigger or better," Domenic replied. "It was fine just the way it was."

"I know."

"I'm going to make him pay for this. Just you wait and see."

"Make who pay?" Matt asked.

"Forsythe," Domenic replied.

"What makes you think he's responsible?"

"I can't talk about it. Not here, not now."

Matt turned to Carla. "Would you mind if Domenic and I took a walk?"

"No," she replied.

Francesca took her grandmother's arm in hers. "Maybe we should do the same," she said.

Matt nodded, pointed. "There's a coffee shop down the street. We'll meet you there in a few minutes."

"Okay," Francesca replied. "Come, Gran," she said. "Let's get you something hot to drink."

Carla nodded, accompanied her granddaughter to the café.

Matt watched them enter the shop, then turned to Domenic. "Tell me exactly what happened. Don't leave anything out."

As they walked along the street, the old man told Matt his story. "Three years ago, this part of Soundview saw a marked increase in the amount of attention it was receiving. Every old building was being acquired by developers. I kept hearing about the offers and the payouts. They were substantial. Many of my friends took the deal they were offered, said it was too good to turn down."

"But you didn't."

Domenic shook his head. "It was never about the money for me. I've made enough to last us for the rest of my life. Carla and I don't want for anything, and although Francesca doesn't know it yet, she will be very a wealthy young woman after we're gone. Carla and I came from nothing. We were both very young when we got married. I was twenty, she was eighteen. We had big dreams, and neither of us was afraid of putting in the hard work to make them come true. Beyond the financial responsibilities that came with raising a family we scrimped and saved and invested every spare nickel we earned. We'd always wanted to own an upscale restaurant. One day, we realized we had set enough aside to make it happen. So, we did. *Vitagliano's* quickly became successful. Pretty soon it was the place to go, not just to dine, but to be seen in. We attracted a who's who of high brow customers. It seemed we could do no wrong. That was before David Forsythe came into our lives."

"What happened then?"

"Another steak house opened close to ours, *Calabriano's*. Virtually the same menu, but more tables and less expensive. From what I've been told, Forsythe is a silent partner in the business."

"You think he's trying to drive you out of business?"

"I know he is."

"What makes you believe that?"

"Because he's doing it all around Soundview. My old neighbors, the businesses on either side of the mission, suddenly began losing money to competitors that seemed to spring up overnight. All were within walking distance of our strip plaza. Donovan's Dry Cleaners and Melissa's Flowers and Baskets? Gone in ten months. Mario's Pizza and Wings and Aretha's Nail Salon? Eight months. Vinnie's Barbershop... Fluff and Fold Laundromat? Six. In every case, their business was literally absorbed. Pretty soon the Guiding Light Mission was the only establishment left in the plaza. Being a non-profit business, we had no competition, so there was nothing financial for us to lose. Still, I couldn't help but feel it was more than a coincidence. Turns out I was right."

"About what?"

"That all the new startups were owned, in whole or in part, by David Forsythe."

"How did you find that out?"

"I went to the city business office, paid a fee, and asked to see the ownership record for each of the new companies. That's when I saw a pattern."

"Pattern?"

Domenic nodded. "All the businesses Forsythe had started were identical to the ventures that had been in our plaza. He drove them all out of business on purpose. Forsythe has no interest in whether the new businesses he started survive. What he wants is the plaza itself, or more specially, the land it sits on."

"So he can develop it."

"Exactly." Domenic pointed to three surrounding buildings. "See those condo towers? They used to be strip plazas too. Care to guess who owns them?"

"David Forsythe."

Domenic nodded. "Same thing happened to the businesses that used to be located where those condos are now. I know because I checked it out. One way or another, Forsythe put them all out of business. And I have a pretty good idea what he's using those new businesses for."

"To wash his drug money."

"Precisely."

Matt stopped, crossed his arms, faced Domenic. "You may be right, but you won't be able to build a case against him on suspicion alone. You'll need proof."

"I know. And that's something I don't have."

"*Yet.*"

"You know something I don't?"

Matt nodded. "Possibly."

"What is it?"

"I'm not prepared to say. I have to do a little digging first."

"Let me help."

Matt shook his head. "No. It's best if you stay off Forsythe's radar right now."

"What are you going to do?"

"Stop him."

"You can't. He's too powerful."

"No one is *too* powerful."

"Why do I get the feeling that whatever you have in mind will be dangerous?"

"Because it will."

Domenic stared at his friend. "Who are you really, Matt?"

"Just a guy trying to make things right."

Domenic smiled. "You've never worked in a restaurant a day in your life, have you?"

Matt cracked a smile. "Was it that obvious?"

"And you're no ex-con or parolee, either. I can spot them a mile away."

"No, I'm not."

"That leaves one thing."

"What's that?"

"You're running from someone... or something."

Matt turned. The two men headed toward the coffee shop where Francesca had taken her grandmother. "Aren't we all?" he replied.

25

Cover

KYLA HID BEHIND a van across the street from the burned-out mission and watched as Matt and the old man walked to the intersection, crossed the road, then entered a coffee shop a few doors down. When it was safe to do so she left her cover position, walked along the street, and observed the café from the shadows. Matt was seated at a table beside the old man. Across from them sat a woman and a teenage girl. The look on the woman's face was solemn, serious. The girl held her hand.

Thirty minutes passed before the group finally rose from their table to leave the café. Matt held the front door open as they exited the establishment, waited with them until their cab arrived, waved as it drove away, then walked back to the intersection, turned the corner, and headed down the street. Kyla waited until Matt was six houses in front of her before she crossed the street and began to follow him. She knew how dangerous a situation this was. Whoever the people were that Matt had just been with, he was comfortable around them. But that was where his trust would end. He was a wanted man, and he knew it. The second he was alone he would again be on high alert, his senses tuned in to the world around him, wary of everything and everyone, ready to respond to the slightest hint of danger or trouble. The CIA had trained him well. He was the most lethal operative she knew. Matt had forgotten more about escape and evade tactics than most field operatives would ever know. He had been responsible for saving their lives while conducting missions on foreign soil on more occasions than she cared to remember. He was a master of the game, which is why her adrenaline spiked when she watched him disappear from view around a distant corner.

Kyla slowed her pace, stepped behind a lamppost, watched, waited. It would be just like Matt to wait her out, then step out from cover and confront her, his weapon at the ready. She maintained her position behind the steel lamppost until she felt it was safe to continue the pursuit, then stepped out from cover. No ambush followed. She was safe, for the moment, but her hesitation had cost her valuable time. She had lost sight of Matt for longer than she was comfortable with. She quickened her pace, reached the alley that Matt had turned down, looked down the dark laneway. All was quiet.

Kyla took no chances. She withdrew the Heckler and Koch pistol from her waistband and held it at her side as she explored the alley.

A rustling sound caught her attention, followed by movement up ahead. She raised the gun, trained it down the nearly lightless service road, then proceeded slowly, scanning the darkness for anything that might give away Matt's presence. She kept her cool, took short, measured steps, evaluated her surroundings, noted nearby opportunities for cover. The steel staircase on her right. The industrial waste bin a few steps ahead. The stack of garbage cans on her left. As she moved past the staircase, the distant threat made itself known. The clattering behind a dumpster thirty feet away was followed by the scurrying away of the largest rat Kyla had ever seen. She watched the animal stop, stare at her inquisitively, then hurry down the alley. Wherever Matt had gone, he had made fast work of exiting the alleyway.

She had lost him.

A lamppost at the far end of the alleyway illuminated the row of townhouses beyond it. He must have gone to one of the units. The question was which one.

Kyla looked up, checked out the roof of the building beside her, listened for sounds above that might indicate that Matt had used the staircase she had passed to make it to high ground. If that was what he had done, and was now watching her from above, she would be a dead woman. He'd have gained the upper hand, and she would find herself in the most dangerous situation of all: an open target, ripe for the killing.

Unnerved by the possibility she could be right, Kyla pointed her weapon up toward the roofline, then pressed her body against the wall of the building and used it for cover.

Before she reached the end of the alleyway, a voice behind her stopped her in her tracks.

"Drop the gun. Hands on your head. Do it now."

Kyla stepped away from the building, dropped the pistol, complied with the command. "Don't shoot, Matt," she said as she raised her hands. "It's me, Kyla."

26

Two Steps Behind

KYLA GLANCED OVER her shoulder, spoke to Matt. "You mind lowering the gun?" she asked. "I didn't come all this way to find you only to get shot."

"Turn around," Matt ordered. "Slowly."

Kyla did as she was told, faced Matt.

Matt kept the gun trained on her as he spoke. "What the hell are you doing here, Kyla? Did Ferriman send you?"

"I asked him for time."

"Time for what?"

"To bring you in."

"How long did he give you?"

"Seventy-two hours."

"And after that?"

"It's open season."

Matt lowered his weapon. "Why you?"

Kyla dropped her hands. "I figured I'd be the one person you'd trust not to kill you."

"I don't."

"How romantic."

"I'm no idiot, Kyla. I know I've been sanctioned. Let me guess... Alpha Level One capture/kill?"

Kyla nodded.

"What makes you think I'll listen to you?"

Kyla smiled. "Because I haven't taken your gun away from you and shot you with it yet." She looked down, pointed to the firearm Matt had ordered her to drop. It lay on the ground beside her. "Mind if I get that?" she asked.

"Yes, I do."

"Seriously, Matt?"

"Kick it over here."

"This is ridiculous."

"*Now.*"

Kyla shook her head, then kicked the pistol across the ground towards Matt. He stopped it with his foot.

"Step back."

Kyla stepped back. "Anyone ever tell you you have serious trust issues?"

"Once or twice."

"They were right."

"On your knees."

"Oh, come on!"

"On the ground, face down."

"You actually think I'm going to rush you?"

"I won't ask twice."

Kyla dropped to her knees, then lay flat on her stomach. "Happy?"

"Ecstatic."

Matt approached her, picked up her weapon, released the clip, ejected the remaining round, caught the bullet in midair as it exited the chamber, then slipped the clip and bullet into his pocket. He stepped around Kyla, knelt, drove his knee into her lower back to control her.

"Jesus!" Kyla said. "Go easy, will ya?"

Matt slipped the operative's empty gun into his waistband as he frisked her. He ran his hands up and down her legs, across her back and neck, down her arms, under her body, checking for additional weapons and spare clips, found nothing. He stood, removed Kyla's gun from his waistband, placed it on the ground at her side. "Get up," he said.

"You sure you don't want to check to see if I'm hiding anything anywhere else while I'm down here? Maybe perform a colonoscopy?"

"Do I need to?"

"No."

"Then we're good."

Kyla stood. "I'm disappointed, Matt. I thought you would have at least given me the benefit of the doubt."

"With my life on the line? Not a chance."

Kyla brushed the dirt from her clothing. "I guess I can't blame you under the circumstances."

"It wouldn't matter if you did."

"I'm not the enemy here, Matt."

"For all I know, that's exactly what you are."

Kyla sighed. "You know that's not true."

"Do I?"

"For God's sake," Kyla urged. "Use a little common sense. If I was the enemy, do you think I'd be here alone? Hell, no. There'd be a team with me. And no matter how good you may think you are, you wouldn't stand a chance. We'd have outflanked you, pushed you into a corner, then aerated your ass. You'd be full of holes and lying dead in front of me right now instead of grilling me like you are."

"Maybe, maybe not."

"Be thankful the situation is what it is."

Matt stared at Kyla, said nothing. She was still as beautiful as he remembered her to be.

"Who were those people you were speaking to in the coffee shop?" she asked.

"Friends."

"Friends? You don't have any friends. That's the tradeoff of our business, remember?"

"This is different."

"Do they know?"

"Know what?"

"Who you are. What you are."

"Of course not."

"You realize you're putting them in danger just by being in your presence, don't you?"

"They have more to be afraid of right now than me."

Kyla paused. "What does that mean?"

"It's not important."

Kyla put out her hand. "Can I have my weapon back?"

"No."

She crossed her arms. "So, what? We're just going to stand here for the rest of the night bantering back and forth while you decide whether or not I came here to kill you?"

"You're the one who's bantering. I'm listening."

"Then listen to this: *I didn't.* Now, do you want my help or not?"

Matt stared into Kyla's eyes, waited for her to flinch,

assessed her body language for signs of deceit, saw none. He slipped his weapon into his waistband, nodded. "I do."

Kyla sighed. "Good. Now buy me a drink and tell me what the hell you're doing here."

Matt pointed. "My place is just down the street."

"You have Scotch?"

"I do."

"Macallan single malt?"

"Naturally."

"Thank God," Kyla said. She walked ahead.

Matt followed, staying two steps behind Kyla.

He kept a wary eye on the street.

27

Nine Roses So Red

DOMENIC, CARLA, AND Francesca exited the cab, approached the stairs in front of their townhouse, then paused. A flower box, wrapped in a bright red bow, stood propped against the door.

Carla turned to her husband. "Honey, did you send me—?"

"No, I didn't," Domenic answered quickly.

"Maybe they're for me!" Francesca exclaimed. She ran up the steps, picked up the box, removed the tiny envelope taped to it, pulled out the card, read it. "Hmm," she said. "This is weird."

"What does the card say?" Domenic asked.

"It says, 'It was a pleasure doing business with you.'" She turned the card over. "There's no name or signature." She looked at her grandfather, shrugged. "What do you suppose it means?"

"Give me the box," Domenic demanded.

"But I want to see what's inside."

"Now, Francesca!"

Francesca handed her grandfather the flower box.

"Both of you walk down the street," Domenic demanded. "After what has happened tonight, I don't want the two of you nearby when I open this."

"You're scaring me, Domenic," Carla said. "You think it might be dangerous?"

"I don't know, and I'm not prepared to take any chances. Now do as I say."

Carla and Francesca followed Domenic's instructions. They hurried back down the steps and along the sidewalk.

Domenic looked at his precious family, issued a firm warning. "No matter what happens, stay there!"

Carla pulled her granddaughter close. "Leave it alone, Domenic," she urged. "If you're that concerned about it put it down and call the police. Let them look at it."

"And tell them what?" Domenic replied. "We received a flower delivery we weren't expecting. Send the bomb squad. Don't be ridiculous."

"Yet you're there and we're here," Carla pressed.

Domenic ignored his wife's comment. He inspected the box from every angle, checked under its lid for wires or anything that looked suspicious, saw nothing, then turned it over. Inside, the contents shifted. He thought for a moment about the suppliers he did business with at the restaurant. The exchange of fruit baskets, bottles of wine, chocolates, and floral bouquets as thank you's for the exchange of favors between one another was common practice among his business associates. But everything about this felt wrong. If this had been a gesture of appreciation, the package would have been delivered to Vitagliano's during regular business hours, not his home, and certainly not at such a late hour.

Francesca called out from the street. "Grandpa, be careful!"

Domenic slipped his hand into his jacket pocket, fished out the pocketknife he always carried with him, opened it. The blade locked into place. Slowly, he passed the sharp edge under the ribbon, cut it carefully, let it fall away from the box. His hand trembled. He took a deep breath, shook off the fear, then lifted the lid.

To his relief, no explosion followed.

Inside the box were a dozen long stem roses. Nine were deep red, exquisite in both their quality and appearance. The remaining three had been stained black.

A second card was nestled in amongst the flowers. Domenic read the words scribbled on it.

Nine roses so red, three black as the night. One too young to die, two too old to fight.

Domenic shuddered at the words and the implied threat that was being sent to him and his family. He slipped the card into his shirt pocket, replaced the lid on the box, marched down the steps to the street, and shoved the macabre flower delivery into a trash can. He waved to his family. "It's all right," he said. "Nothing to be concerned about. Probably just some kids playing a prank." He pointed to the front door. "Everyone inside. Let's go."

"What was it?" Carla asked.

"Nothing to be worried about," he replied.

"You didn't answer Gran's question," Francesca said.

"Just a flower delivery," Domenic replied.

"You're not keeping them?"

"No."

"Why not?" Francesca pressed.

"Because I'm not," Domenic answered firmly. "And that's all either of you need to know. End of discussion."

"It was from them, wasn't it?" Francesca said. "The Diamondbacks."

Domenic was losing patience with his granddaughter. "Even if it was, it's not your concern. My dealings with the Diamondbacks, whatever they may be, are mine and mine alone. Now go inside the house."

"What do you mean, not my concern? If it concerns you and grandma, it concerns me!"

Domenic inserted his key, unlocked the front door, pushed it open. "Young lady, you must be really eager to get grounded."

"Of course I'm not."

"Then I suggest you drop the matter right now and high-tail it inside."

Francesca stared at her grandfather, then stormed into the house and ran upstairs to her room.

From the bottom of the staircase, Domenic and Carla heard her bedroom door slam shut. Seconds later, music blared from inside her room.

"She's just upset over what happened tonight," Carla said. "I'll talk to her in a minute and calm her down."

"All right," Domenic replied. "I'll be in my study. Call out if you need me."

"I will." Carla touched her husband's face with her palm. "Be honest with me, Domenic," she said. "Are we in danger?"

Domenic shook his head. "You have nothing to be afraid of, sweetheart. I promise. It's nothing I can't handle."

"Are you sure?"

"One hundred percent."

Carla stared into her husband's kind eyes, believed him. "Okay," she said.

Domenic smiled, pointed upstairs. "Tell our fiercely independent granddaughter to turn down the music or, at the very least, play something decent. I hate that rap crap."

Carla smiled. "Hey, you agreed to the rules. Her room, her music."

"Don't remind me."

Carla headed up the stairs. "I'll be down in a minute. Pour me a glass of wine?"

"Cab sauv?"

"Please."

Domenic waited for his wife to enter Francesca's room and close the door before he hurried to his study, opened the closet doors, knelt on the floor, then removed the small metal box he kept hidden in the back corner under a stack of old sweaters. From the pocket of one of the garments he withdrew a key, slipped it into the box's lock, opened it, then removed the weapon his wife never knew he kept in the house: a Walther PPK semi-automatic handgun, fully loaded.

Domenic closed and locked the box, buried it once more beneath the sweaters, then stood, slipped the gun into his pocket, and walked to the front door. He called out. "Carla."

The door to Francesca's room opened. The music had been turned down to an acceptable level. Calmness, it seemed, had been restored.

Carla stepped into the hall and looked down at her husband standing in the vestibule. "Yes, hon."

"I have to step out for a minute. I'll be back soon."

"Where are you going?"

"The store. We need milk."

"Can it wait?"

Domenic shook his head. "You know how Francesca gets if she doesn't have her cereal in the morning."

Carla smiled. "All right, but be careful. It's late."

"I will."

As Domenic stepped out the door, the words on the card accompanying the bizarre flower delivery whirled about in his mind. The thought of anyone threatening his family was more than he could bear. He had no choice. He knew who was responsible. He had to put an end to this.

And he had to do it tonight.

28

Mantra

D AVID FORSYTHE DREAMED of celebratory ribbon-cutting ceremonies, business awards and presentations, and burned-out buildings. The subconscious images had appeared so vividly in his mind and felt so real that they had pulled him out of a deep, restful sleep. In the darkness of his fortieth-floor penthouse suite he opened his eyes, stared up at the ceiling, and recalled his earlier conversation with Martine from Gentry Fine Cigars.

It was done.

By now, the Guiding Light Mission would have been reduced to smoldering rubble. What was left of it would be demolished following the completion of the fire marshal's investigation. The authorities would find nothing, of course. That was why he paid Gentry the exorbitant amount that he did. Martine guaranteed his work. His people were all ex-military, his arsonists professionals. There would be no residue, no specific point of origin, nothing to identify the cause of the blaze or the ensuing explosion. Most importantly, there would be nothing to tie him to the crime.

The desire to see for himself the result of their work was compelling. He had to go to the Mission now.

Forsythe rolled over in bed, retrieved his cell phone from his side table, placed a call.

"Good morning, Mr. Forsythe."

David Forsythe was not a man to exchange pleasantries with his underlings. "Prepare my car and notify my security detail," he said. "I'll be downstairs in fifteen minutes."

"Yes, s—"

Forsythe ended the call. He turned to the woman lying in bed beside him, pushed her with his hand. "Get up," he said. "You need to leave."

The woman stirred, wiped the sleep from her eyes. "What time is it?" she asked.

"Never mind. Just get your things and go."

"Did I do something wrong?"

"No."

"Then why—"

"Because I fucking well said so, that's why!"

The woman sat up in bed. "All right," she replied. "No need to be rude."

Forsythe opened his nightstand, removed his wallet, pulled out ten crisp one-hundred-dollar bills, tossed them on the bed. The money fluttered down, landing on both the woman and his expensive Egyptian cotton fitted sheets. "That's a grand. Leave your number with the front desk. I'll call you."

The woman pulled the sheets up to her neck. "I'm not a professional," she said, offended at the thought that Forsythe had taken her to be a prostitute.

"Could've fooled me."

The woman threw back the sheets, hurried out of bed, collected her clothes off the floor, dressed quickly. "Asshole," she said.

Forsythe smiled, ignored the insult. "You need a ride home?"

"No!"

"Suit yourself."

The woman stormed past the drug lord turned real estate mogul and out of the bedroom. Forsythe followed her, waited as the elevator dinged announcing its arrival, watched her enter the lift, then give him the finger as its doors closed. He smiled at the gesture, then returned to his bedroom to dress. "Girl's got spunk," he said aloud. He glanced at the bed and the money laying atop the sheets. "No business sense, but spunk for days."

He collected the cash, returned it to his wallet, walked to his closet, made his selection from one of a dozen Tom Ford suits, dress shirts, belts, and shoes, chose a watch from his collection - a Cartier Ballon Bleu, white gold and covered in diamonds – and dressed. He checked his look in the mirror, ruffled his hair, smoothed in a little gel, brushed his teeth, splashed his face with cold water, grabbed his favorite over-coat from the hall closet, then left the bedroom, walked to the elevator, pressed the call button, and waited for the lift to arrive.

He rode the car down to the lobby. On reaching the first floor, he looked ahead, saw his white Lincoln Navigator parked under the portico, its rear door open and awaiting his arrival, guarded by a member of his three man security detail.

Forsythe strode through the lobby of the building he owned, eager to begin the brief journey to the gravesite of the Guiding Light Mission. It had been a shame that he had to resort to such extreme measures to force the old man and his family out of the premises. But that had been on him. He had tried to pay him off, but Vitagliano would have none of it. Now he was left with exactly nothing. So be it. *When generosity fails, let greed prevail.* It was this mantra to which he attributed his business success. The death of the mission was one of many to come. If all went according to plan, within five years he would be the richest man in Soundview. Within ten, The Bronx itself. Men like Vitagliano were nothing more than a nuisance, a temporary obstacle. By utilizing the services of the right people at the right time, like the good folks at Gentry Fine Cigars, no obstacle would remain in his path for long.

The bodyguard saw his boss coming, raised his hand. Forsythe stopped just inside the entrance to the building and waited. This was protocol. After conducting a final threat assessment of the condominium grounds by his security team, the bodyguard ushered him into the back seat of his bulletproof vehicle.

The bodyguard opened the front passenger door, took a seat inside, closed it. "Destination, sir?" he asked.

"The Guiding Light Mission," Forsythe replied.

"Yes, sir."

The driver waited for the third member of the team to take his place in the back seat beside his boss before pulling away from the front entrance.

Ten minutes to the Mission.

29

Pull Strength

"THIS IS ME," Matt said to Kyla as they reached his townhouse. He scanned the street before walking up the steps.

"What are you looking for?" Kyla asked.

"What do you think?"

"I told you, Matt. I'm alone. At least for the time being."

"What is that supposed to mean?"

"That we need to talk. But first, I want that drink you promised me." She pointed to Matt's front door. "Are we going in or staying out here?"

Matt extended his hand. Kyla walked up the steps ahead of him. Matt met her at the door, unlocked it, waited for her to enter ahead of him.

"Still not going to let me out of your sight, huh?" Kyla asked.

Matt shrugged. "I'm cautious that way."

Kyla nodded. "Whatever makes you comfortable." She spied the bar cart in the corner of Matt's living room. "You mind?" she asked.

Matt shook his head. "Help yourself."

Kyla crossed the room, took a glass from a tray on the brass cart, opened the bottle of Macallan, poured herself a shot. "Are you joining me?" she asked.

Matt nodded. He crossed the room, stood beside her as she poured his drink, then took the glass from her hand.

Kyla lifted her glass, sipped the smooth spirit. "Excellent," she said.

Matt downed the shot, placed the empty glass on the bar cart, pointed to the couch. "Have a seat," he said.

Kyla walked to the sofa, sat, looked around. "Nice digs," she said. "Why come here?"

"You know why. I like Soundview. Plus, I had a gut feeling if anyone would come looking for me first it would be you. The ink's barely dry on Ferriman's C/K order and here you are with no backup, or so you claim."

"I'm alone, Matt. I promise."

Matt walked across the living room, seated himself in a bucket chair across from Kyla. He removed his gun from his waistband, placed it on the table beside him.

"You won't be needing that anymore," Kyla said. "I have no intention of killing you."

"So you say."

"Besides, my weapon is altogether useless to me now. No clip, remember?"

Matt reached into his pocket, withdrew the clip he had ejected from Kyla's gun, relieved the magazine of its bullets, thumbing out one round at a time into a candy dish on the table beside him. When the clip was empty he tossed it across the room. Kyla caught it in her hand. "There you go," he said. "You have your clip back."

"I would have preferred it with bullets."

"I'm sure you would."

Kyla let out a heavy sigh. "Why did you do it, Matt?"

"Do what?"

"Belie an order so important that you ended up in the middle of this bullshit."

"Because I'm a professional, not a killer."

"There's a difference?"

"To me there is."

"I read your package details. You had a clear line of sight and the target in view, yet you didn't take the shot. Why?"

"His kid was with him."

"So?"

"It wasn't necessary."

"Not necessary? Jesus, Matt! That's Ferriman's decision to make, not yours."

"That's not how I see it."

"Then let me enlighten you. You're the tip of the spear, the four-and-a-half-pound pull strength needed to draw the trigger. That's it. Nothing more, nothing less. You don't get to have an opinion on the matter. Nothing about *you* factors into the equation, not even remotely. You have been sanctioned by your government to do one job and one job only with total impunity: to take someone's life whenever and wherever you're ordered you to do so."

"It's that easy for you, is it?"

"Yes, Matt. It is. It's the job we signed up for and one we're both good at. There's a reason so few of us get to operate in the field at this level. We've proven that we have the mental, physical, and emotional stamina to do the job. The second you begin to insert your own feelings into the mix it's time to pack it up. Is that where you are now? Are you done?"

"I'm not sure."

"Well, you better get sure real fast. The clock is running out on you. Ferriman must harbor some hope that you're worth saving, otherwise it wouldn't be me sitting here. I'm your best chance for a second chance. That is, if you want it."

"And what if I don't? What if I am done?"

"Then I suggest you run like hell. Get as far away from here as you can. If you have contacts abroad that can drop you deep into a country somewhere off the grid, reach out to them and disappear. But know this. If that's the route you choose to go, it's a one-way ticket. There'll be no coming back from that decision after you've made it. And with all you've seen and done and all you know, you won't be able to stop running. You know the agency. They won't let up, ever. It will only be a matter of time before someone finds you and puts one in your head and one in your heart. Is that really how you want to end your career?"

Matt shook his head. "No."

"Then let me make the call. I'll tell Ferriman I've found you and that you've agreed to come in. You'll have to stand before a board of inquiry and be asked to defend your actions, which we both know they won't accept. Best-case scenario? You'll ride a desk for the rest of your career. Worst case is you'll be forced to leave the agency. But who cares? You're still young enough to start over if you want to. Maybe even go back to Baylor and teach Poly Sci. My point is this. If you work with me now, you have a chance. If you don't, you won't. It's that simple."

Matt stared at Kyla, considered all she had just said to him. He appreciated her honesty, could hear it in her voice. Most importantly, he knew she was right. She was his only option now.

"All right," Matt said. "I'll turn myself in."

Kyla smiled. "Thank you, Matt. You're making the right decision."

"But with one condition."

"I'm trying to save your life here, Matt. You're in no position to be adding conditions."

"Are you going to hear me out or not?"

"What is it?"

"The people you saw me speaking with in the café. They're in trouble. They need help."

"And you want to help them?"

"I do."

"And if I say no?"

"Then that little motivational speech you just gave was a complete waste of time."

Kyla smiled. "I can work with that." She raised her empty glass. "You mind?"

Matt pointed to the bar cart. "Help yourself."

Kyla stood. "After this, I could really use a shower. Mind if I borrow yours?"

Matt smiled. "Not at all."

30

Push It Down

A S DOMENIC WALKED up the street, he became aware of the hard object pressing into the small of his back. The presence of the gun felt foreign to him. Stupid, he thought. He was not a killer. He would never be capable of drawing the weapon on another individual, much less shooting and killing them out of anger. He had purchased the weapon for home defense in the event of a break-in. As an older man, he was painfully aware that his age and physical limitations would not work in his favor should one night his peaceful home be invaded by crackhead teenagers or criminals decades his junior. He thought about Carla's words. *The insurance company will cover the loss.* She was right. She was also right when she had said that if they needed to they would use some of their own money to rebuild the Guiding Light Mission and make it better than it was before the fire. Still, he couldn't get the image of the incinerated shell out of his mind. How could the blaze have burned so hot to have done the damage it did in such a short period of time before the fire department arrived? It had to have been arson. There was no other logical explanation. He needed to tour the remains and investigate the scene for himself. Not that he had any level of expertise in fire causation. He didn't. But what he had was a keen eye and an excellent memory. He knew every square inch of the mission. Incinerated or not, if something was out of place, he was confident he would see it. If he was successful in locating a foreign object in the wreckage he would take the evidence to the police, who would hand it over to the fire department's investigators. The experts would take it from there.

When he reached the intersection, the smell of burning metal still hung heavily in the air. Although the fire had been extinguished and posed no further risk of reigniting from within the rubble, the wreckage still smoldered as the metal cooled. Domenic stepped through what had been the entrance to the mission. Wisps of smoke rose from the debris, snaked around his feet, dissipated. He walked through the cremains of the building, viewed the carnage. Folding plastic banquet tables which had once hosted dozens of needy guests for breakfast, lunch, and dinner now lay melted on the ground, their steel legs the sole survivors of the intense heat. Overturned chairs, pushed aside by the firefighters as they fought to subdue the blaze, dotted the floor. Above him, the ceiling and most of the second floor was gone. The steel staircase that once led up to the second floor now stood on its own, a bridge to nowhere.

Domenic made his way to the back of the building and the location of his former office. Along the way he passed the serving counter, smelled the sickly-sweet aroma emanating from hundreds of tiny self-serve packets of ketchup, mustard, relish, mayonnaise, and sugar that had cooked in their packaging from the intense heat. The steel dishwashing station remained relatively intact but now served only to support stacks of heat cracked ceramic plates, cups, and saucers. In the food storage room, which had served as his office, nothing remained. His desk and chair were gone, as was every food item which had once sat on the shelf. The commercial refrigerator and freezer had been ruined and were no longer usable. Domenic opened the door to both units and checked their contents, hoping to salvage some of the items and send them to neighboring food banks. No luck. The heat from the fire had melted their airtight seals. The blaze had found a path inside and cooked the goods. The stench of the burnt food was over-powering and took him off guard. He turned away, thought he might retch, but managed to control himself and push it down.

From inside the kitchen, he stared out at the dark street beyond the building. Outside, a vehicle slowed to a stop.

Domenic suddenly realized he had no right to be wandering around inside the remains of the building. He had seen the sign posted by the fire marshal's office prohibiting access to the site when he had approached the wreckage, but curiosity had gotten the better of him. Besides, to his way of thinking, he had every right to be here. For years, together with his wife and granddaughter, he had tended to the mission. Together they had made it the success it had become. Losing the Mission felt no different to him than if it had been his own home which had burned to the ground. The pain felt just as raw, cut just as deep.

Domenic turned his attention back to the street. The vehicle which had just arrived, a large white SUV, looked very official. Perhaps investigators from the insurance company or fire marshal's office had arrived to do a final walkthrough of the building in order to complete their reports. He debated whether he should step out from behind the small section of wall that remained standing in the scorched dishwashing station area and present himself to the officials or remain hidden. Perhaps he would learn more if he stayed out of sight and eavesdropped on their conversation. Yes, this was the best course of action. Proprietor or not, they would not likely be willing to share their knowledge or suspicions with him at this early stage of their investigation.

The vehicle's door opened. The driver exited and was joined by a second man. The men scanned the street, searched it in both directions. From Domenic's limited perspective, their body language indicated that they were standing guard. The two were soon joined by a third man, who appeared at the rear of the SUV, then stepped out of sight. Domenic watched the dome light illuminate inside the vehicle, then go out. The final passenger walked around the vehicle. Under the soft light of a streetlamp above the blacked-out SUV, Domenic recognized him. His heart suddenly began to race, his breath to quicken.

David Forsythe and his bodyguards had arrived at the Mission.

Domenic tried to push down his welling rage but couldn't. Unconsciously, his hand found the grip of the weapon tucked into his waistband.

He pulled out the gun, held it at his side, then waited for the men to enter the grave of the once proud sanctuary for the homeless.

31

Unicorn

KYLA STEPPED OUT of the shower, toweled off. In his bedroom, Matt had placed his housecoat on the bed for her. Kyla let the damp towel drop to the floor. She slipped into the warm terrycloth robe, wrapped it around her, then walked into the den. She found the rogue agent sitting at his desk in front of his laptop. A cell phone was connected to the machine. Matt was reading the information on the computer screen.

"What's that?" Kyla asked.

Matt looked up, saw her standing beside him. Kyla ran her fingers through her damp hair, tousled it. He smiled, shook his head.

Kyla noticed his reaction when he looked at her. "What?" she said.

"Nothing."

"It's not nothing. Spill."

"It's you."

"Me?"

"Yeah."

"What about me?"

"You haven't changed a bit."

"Meaning?"

"You're still as drop dead gorgeous as I remember you to be."

Kyla smiled, placed her hand on his shoulder. "Thank you. I'm glad you think so."

Matt pointed to the bullets in the candy dish beside his chair. "Take them," he said.

Kyla smiled. "Is this your definition of a peace offering?"

Matt shrugged. "We both know that if you really wanted me dead, a bullet wouldn't be your only option."

"True," Kyla replied.

"Besides, if they gave me a preference for whom I'd want to take me out, I'd pick you."

"I'm not here to kill you, Matt. Quite the opposite. I'm here to save your life."

Matt nodded. "I know that now."

"Good," Kyla said. She looked over his shoulder. "What are you doing?"

"Hacking into a cell phone I took off a kid."

"I recognize that software. Unicorn, right?"

Matt nodded.

"That's only available to analysts, not field operatives. How did you get it?"

"Long story."

"I've got time."

Matt smiled. "I saved the CEO's life while on his protection detail in Israel. He insisted on repaying me, so I asked him to hook me up with a back door key to his software, which he did."

"You're not going through the agency's server?"

Matt shook his head. "No. I'm connected directly to Unicorn."

"So, you're a hacker now?"

Matt smiled. "Hardly. Just curious."

"About what?"

"Not *what*. Who."

"Who?"

"Whoever was responsible for setting the fire that took out the Guiding Light Mission."

"Why would that be important to you?"

"It just is."

"Would this have anything to do with the people I saw you speaking with at the coffee shop?"

Matt nodded.

"What's the connection?"

"They're names are Domenic, Carla, and Francesca Vitagliano. They operated the mission. Domenic told me he's been having trouble with a gang that's taking over Soundview. They call themselves the Diamondbacks. According to Domenic, they've been pressuring local business owners to sell out and relocate."

"Why would they want to do that?"

"They don't. The head of the Diamondbacks is a real estate developer by the name of David Forsythe. Seems he wants to tear down all the strip plazas in Soundview and erect condominiums in their place."

"I take it the Vitagliano's refused to play along."

"That's right."

"And the phone?"

"There was a kid in the crowd who looked out of place. I watched him for a few minutes, then followed him. When he left the scene I bumped him, took his phone."

"Why him?"

"I overheard part of his conversation. It sounded like he was relaying a message to whoever wanted the mission taken out, telling them that the job had been done."

"And you think that person is David Forsythe?"

Matt nodded.

"Did Unicorn find anything on the kid's phone to confirm your suspicion?"

"Big time," Matt said. He clicked an icon on the screen labeled TRANSCRIPT, then pointed to the screen. "Check it out."

Kyla read Unicorn's voice-to-screen transcription between the kid's phone and the last number he had called. The conversation between David Forsythe and Benny Ortiz, the kid's real name as associated with the cell phone account, implied that Benny had been there to be David Forsythe's eyes on the scene. His job was to report back to him on the damage that had been done to the mission and whether or not the blaze had been successful.

"Jesus," Kyla said. "You think Forsythe had the mission burned down just to get the property?"

Matt nodded. "That, and more."

"What do you mean?"

"The Diamondbacks and David Forsythe have their fingers in more than one pie. They're heavy into drug dealing and distribution, specifically their own brand of crack cocaine. They call it Sapphire Slam. They're trying to recruit the less fortunate in the area to sell it for them on the street."

Kyla shook her head. "This guy sounds like a real piece of work."

"He is. But he won't be for much longer."

"What do you plan to do?"

"Tear his world apart."

"I don't know, Matt. He seems like a pretty dangerous dude."

"So am I."

"Who, if he doesn't play his cards right, will soon become the target of a nationwide manhunt."

Matt nodded. "I know. But I can't let this go."

"You mean *won't* let this go."

"That's right."

"So, what's next?"

Matt wrote down Benny Ortiz's home address. "I'm going to pay this kid a visit and ask him to tell me everything he knows about Forsythe and his operation."

"And if he doesn't?"

"That won't be an option."

Kyla sighed. "You really want this guy, don't you?"

Matt nodded. "Yeah, I do."

She turned Matt's chair around, faced him. "All right. I'll help you take down Forsythe. But I'm going to need you to do something for me in return."

"What's that?"

Kyla untied the belt, let the robe fall open. "Help me out of this."

Matt pulled her close. "I think I can manage to do that."

Kyla giggled. "Oh, I know you can."

32

Ten Minutes

CARLA STOOD ON the front steps of her walk-up townhouse, drew her sweater tightly around her body, glanced up and down the street, searched for her husband. Domenic was nowhere in sight.

This made no sense. He had told her he was going to the corner store to pick up milk for Francesca. The store was a five minute walk away, ten minutes round trip. Forty-five minutes had passed and still no Domenic.

She knew he was having a terrible time dealing with the loss of the mission, as were they all. Perhaps he had extended his walk, taken an indirect route there and back, used the extra time to clear his mind and shake off the anger he felt about losing that which had meant so much to him. She hoped she'd gotten through to him, made him realize that the fire that had taken the mission had not taken his dream with it, and that in due course they would be able to resume the good work they were doing in a bigger and better facility. But she was also acutely aware of how stubborn and single-minded her husband was. She had seen the fire in his eyes, heard the anger in his voice. What Domenic wanted now more than anything else was for someone to be held accountable for the destruction of the mission. She could give him a shoulder to lean on and all the sensible advice in the world, but she knew that when he was in this state there was nothing she could say or do that would be enough to calm him down. This was something he had to work out for himself. If an extra-long walk would be enough to diffuse his anxiety, then so be it. She would wait it out. They would talk when he returned if that was what he wanted to do. Being married for a very long time meant she knew when it was wise to engage him in conversation and when it was best to simply let him be. Domenic was a proud man who had worked very hard for the success he had achieved in his life. He was also a fighter, and at this moment, it was that character trait that most worried her.

Francesca called out from inside the house. "Gran, you okay?"

Carla replied. "I'm fine, honey."

Her granddaughter bounded down the stairs, opened the screen door, stepped outside, joined her on the steps. "Grandpa's not back yet?"

Carla shook her head. "No."

"I thought he was just going to the store for milk."

"That's what he said he was doing."

"You don't suppose he went back to the mission, do you?"

"Why would he do that? There's nothing there for him to be concerned about anymore."

"Want me to go check on him?"

Carla shook her head. "It's best to give him some space right now. He'll come home when he's ready."

Francesca nodded. "I suppose."

Carla turned to her granddaughter. "You should go to bed, honey. You have classes in the morning."

Francesca objected. "You don't expect me to go to school tomorrow after all that's happened tonight?"

"Yes, I do," Carla replied. "And so will your grandfather. You know how important it is to him that you do well in school."

"School sucks. It's boring. I can sleep through class and still get straight A's."

"And we know why that is, right?"

"Yes, ma'am."

"What is it that your grandfather is always reminding you of?"

"That I'm gifted."

"And?"

"That high school is just a steppingstone."

"To?"

"Harvard."

"For?"

"Medicine."

"Why?"

"Because I've wanted to become a doctor ever since I was a kid."

"Exactly."

Francesca gave her grandmother a hug. "You know I worry about you and grandpa, right?"

Carla smiled. "I know you do, dear."

"This whole thing with the mission. It's got to be tearing him up inside."

Carla nodded. "It is. But your grandfather is a pretty tough cookie. We've weathered worse storms than this. We'll get through it like we have the others."

"I hope so."

"I know so."

Francesca ran down the steps.

"Where are you going?" Carla asked.

The teen lifted the lid off the garbage can, removed the box of flowers Domenic had thrown out. "Getting these!" she said.

She returned to the top of the stairs, opened the box, folded back the white tissue paper, revealed the bouquet. "What the heck?" she said.

Carla shivered when she saw the three black roses mixed among the nine red flowers.

"Why would someone send us flowers like this?" Francesca said. "This doesn't look right."

Carla tried to hide her fear. "I don't know, honey. Perhaps it's like your grandfather said. Someone's idea of a bad joke."

Francesca examined the red roses. "Pretty expensive joke if you ask me." She ran her fingers across the black rose petals, examined them in the soft porch light. "These have been stained," she said. "Have you ever seen anything like this before?"

Carla shook her head. "Never."

Francesca searched the box, found the card that had been taped to the lid, read it again: *Nice doing business with you*. "This was no joke," she said. "These were delivered to grandpa on purpose."

"Leave it alone, Francesca. We have enough to be concerned about with the mission right now. These flowers are the least of our concern."

"I think someone is trying to intimidate grandpa," the teen said. "And I'll bet I know who it is."

"That's enough. Your grandfather told you once before that this was none of your concern. Now I'm telling you, too. Put them back in the trash where they belong."

"But Gran!"

"Now, Francesca."

Francesca did as she was told. "You're keeping something from me, aren't you?"

"This is a matter for adults to deal with, not a teenager."

"I know someone who could get to the bottom of this in a hurry."

"No one's getting to the bottom of anything, Francesca."

"Matt could."

Carla's tone was curt, to the point. "This is a family matter, young lady. You will say nothing about this to Matt. Do you understand me?"

Francesca acquiesced. "With the Mission burned down, I guess there's no reason for him to come around anymore, right?"

"That's right."

"How long has grandpa been gone now?"

Carla checked her watch. "One hour."

"We both know what that means. Grandpa wasn't going to the store to buy milk."

"That's where he said he was going," Carla replied nervously.

Francesca crossed her arms. "Then why is there an unopened container in the fridge?"

Carla stared at her granddaughter. She hadn't thought to check the fridge, saw no reason to do so. "I didn't know there was."

"Well, there is," Francesca replied. "I'm giving him ten minutes to come home. If he's not back by then, I'm going to look for him."

"You'll do no such thing."

Francesca stared at her grandmother. "I love you, Gran," she said. "But yes, I am."

33

Click

DAVID FORSYTHE STOPPED to appreciate the extent of the destruction the firebombing had done to the mission. "Beautiful," he said.

The men crossed the street, entered the burned-out shell of the building.

"Jesus, talk about fried," the driver said.

As one of Forsythe's bodyguards entered the structure, a second held him back. "It might not be wise for you to go in there, sir," he said. "It looks pretty unstable."

Forsythe looked at the man, stared down at the hand on his arm.

The bodyguard released his grip.

Forsythe stared at him. "Don't ever try to think for me again," he said. "Got it?"

"Yes, sir," he replied. "My apologies."

Forsythe walked ahead, entered the structure. The destruction around him was complete. He knew when he had contracted with Gentry that he had hired the best in the business, but he had no idea they would be this thorough. Only the mission had been taken out by the blaze. The vacant shops on either side of the unit had not been touched. The firebombs had been perfectly placed to ensure maximum annihilation to the target but leave the adjoining units intact. The concrete firewalls between the three units had done their job by successfully containing the blaze and stopping it from crossing over. The second floor was another story. It was completely gone. Forsythe looked up at the night sky above. The moonless night added to the eerie ambiance, kept the mission cloaked in shadows. A rat ran across the floor. It appeared that even in death the building had found a new and equally noble purpose: to provide safe harbor for the creatures of the night.

Forsythe's driver watched the rodent scurry across the floor and dart under a pile of rubble, only to reappear seconds later in another section of the building. He removed his pistol, pointed it at the rat.

"Are you out of your mind?" Forsythe asked. "Put that away!"

The driver holstered the gun. "Sorry, boss," he said. "I hate those fucking things."

"Do something stupid like that again and I'll toss it in a bag and throw it over your head," Forsythe replied.

"Understood, boss," the man said. "It won't happen again."

Forsythe's second bodyguard had ventured further into

the building. He stood at the foot of the staircase to nowhere, looked up. "Man," he said. "This place must have burned at one hell of a temperature to have taken out the second floor like that." He glanced at his boss. "Any idea what caused the blaze, sir?"

"None," Forsythe lied. "It's an old plaza. Bad wiring, maybe. These structures still use old style electrical. I wouldn't be surprised if a short caused a spark and it spread from there."

The driver nodded. "Could be. Seems strange, though."

"What does?" Forsythe asked.

"How thoroughly it burned."

"What do you mean?"

"I've seen my share of burned-out buildings when I served overseas. Hell, I even took out a few of them myself. This looks different."

"Different how?"

The driver shrugged. "It's nothing."

Forsythe insisted. "I asked you how it looks different. Tell me."

The driver nodded. "If I was back in Afghanistan and seeing this for the first time, the last thing I'd think of would be an electrical short. It looks like someone took a flamethrower to this place. This was no slow burn. This happened fast, instantaneously, like a firebomb went off in here. You got any enemies who'd want to do this to you, boss? To burn the place down, I mean?"

Forsythe shook his head.

"Could have been kids," the driver speculated. "The L Street Crew's been making waves lately, trying to expand their operation across the river into Soundview. Maybe this was them taking a poke at you, trying to see what kind of reaction they'd get, maybe hoping to start a turf war. Fire-bombing one of your strip malls would be a good way to stir something up."

Placing the blame on a rival street gang suddenly struck Forsythe as a good idea. It would offer him plausible denia-bility if questions arose about the cause of the blaze. Gang violence was a concern in Soundview. If the fire marshal's investigators were lucky enough to find something that looked suspicious, he would offer that as a possible reason. He would still have to explain why a plaza he owned had been targeted, and just how much of a coincidence it was that the mission was the last remaining business in the plaza. But that was an issue for his attorneys to deal with. It was for that reason and more he kept the city's best law firm on retainer.

Forsythe's bodyguard walked towards what had formerly been the establishment's kitchen. A partial wall was all that remained of the rear area of the building. He called out seconds later. "Boss."

Forsythe stood beside his driver, looking up, still taking in the gaping view of the night sky through the open space between the adjoining units. "Yes?" he replied.

"We have a problem."

Forsythe turned, looked towards the kitchen area. "What kind of a prob—"

The bodyguard slowly stepped out from behind the broken wall.

Domenic stood behind him, holding him by his collar, his gun pressed against the back of the man's head.

Forsythe stepped ahead. "Mr. Vitagliano," he said. "What are you doing here at such a late hour?"

Domenic's voice shook. "You sonofabitch," he replied. "Why did you do it?"

Forsythe shook his head. "I'm afraid you have me at a disadvantage. Why did I do what?"

"Destroy the mission."

Forsythe shrugged. "I don't know what you're talking about."

"You know *exactly* what I'm talking about!" Domenic yelled.

"Easy," Forsythe replied. "You might want to keep your voice down. You wouldn't want to draw attention to yourself, especially while you're holding a gun to my associate's head. The floor is covered in debris. You might stumble. It could go off by mistake. And that would create a problem for both of us."

"Fine if it does. There'd be one less scumbag in the world."

"That's a grossly unfair assessment of a man you don't even know."

"If he's associated with you, it's not."

While Forsythe engaged the old man in conversion, his second bodyguard took advantage of the situation and positioned himself in another part of the building. He removed his gun, held it at his side, watched as Domenic moved further into the middle of the fallen structure.

"Do you know what you've done?" Domenic asked.

Forsythe feigned ignorance. "Done, Mr. Vitagliano? I don't understand."

"What you've taken away from my family and the people who relied on the services we provided?"

"There are many services for the poor and destitute. Your little mission was nothing special."

"It was to us and the people who came here every day."

Forsythe began to close the distance between himself and Domenic. "Do you want the chance to continue doing your good work?" he asked.

"Of course, I do."

"Then you're going about it all wrong."

"Stay back," Domenic said. He pressed the gun harder against the man's skull.

"Don't be a fool, Mr. Vitagliano," Forsythe said. "You're no killer. Not even close. If I were to guess, I'd say you've never even held a gun before in your life, much less fired one. Am I right?"

"Don't come any closer!" Domenic warned.

Forsythe had closed the gap. Only a few feet remained between them. He held out his hand. "Give me the gun, Mr. Vitagliano."

"No!" Domenic replied.

The second bodyguard had narrowed the distance between himself and Domenic. Forsythe looked at him and nodded.

Behind him, Domenic heard a distinct *click* as the man pulled back the weapon's hammer. He froze. He was in way over his head. Forsythe was right. Other than taking the gun out of his lockbox to clean it now and then, he had never handled a weapon before. The thought of having his finger on the trigger of a loaded weapon frightened him. He could never pull the trigger. Despite how much he despised Forsythe and his men, he could never take a life. It would do nothing to solve his problem, now or ever.

Domenic relented. He lowered the gun, held it at his side.

His hostage stepped away, then quickly turned and punched him in the face.

Domenic fell to his knees, dropped the weapon.

The man bent down, picked up the gun. "Point a gun at me, you fucking asshole?" he said. He pressed the pistol against Domenic's forehead. "I should cap your geriatric ass right here and now!"

"Enough!" Forsythe said. "Give me the gun."

The man fumed, shook his head. "No fucking way!"

Forsythe looked at his second bodyguard standing behind Domenic, nodded. The man understood. He raised his weapon, pointed it at his associate. "You heard what the boss said. Do it."

The gunman looked at his colleague, stared down the barrel of his weapon.

His associate spoke again. "It's a no-win situation. You kill him, I kill you. You really want that?"

The bodyguard held his gaze, then lowered the gun and stepped away from Domenic.

"Wise move," his partner said, then lowered his weapon.

Forsythe addressed the two men. "Take him. Put him in the car."

Domenic allowed himself to be taken by his arm and escorted out of the remains of the Guiding Light Mission.

"You're a fool, Vitagliano," Forsythe said as his bodyguards and driver escorted Domenic out of the building to the waiting SUV. "All you had to do was take my offer. Now we have a real problem on our hands, don't we?"

The driver opened the vehicle's rear passenger door, motioned for Domenic to get in.

Domenic climbed into the back seat. "What problem is that?" he asked.

Forsythe slipped in beside him. "What to do with you."

The driver started the car, checked his mirrors, then pulled away from the curb.

Behind them two rats scurried across the street into the mission.

34

Reason To Believe

MATT AND KYLA lay in bed. She ran her fingers across his chest. "I've missed this," she said. "More to the point, I've missed you."

"Me too," Matt replied.

"I reached out to you twice. Picked up the phone, dialed your number. You even answered once."

"Why didn't you say anything?"

Kyla shrugged. "I guess I was scared."

"Of what?"

"The thought of *us*."

"That's supposed to turn you on, not off."

"I mean the thought of there being an us again, only to lose you like I did last time."

"It's this job," Matt said. "It leaves no time for a personal life. Relationships just make matters more complicated."

"Have you ever thought about me?"

Matt nodded. "All the time."

"Really?"

He leaned over, opened his bedside table drawer, removed a small silver box, handed it to her.

"What's this?" she asked.

"Open it."

Kyla sat up, opened the tiny box. Inside she found a dozen loose emeralds. She picked out a stone, examined it in the light. "It's beautiful," she said. "Where did you get them?"

"Columbia."

"They look expensive."

"They are."

"Did you buy them as an investment?"

"You could say that."

"What do you mean?"

"I bought them for you. I was going to have a bracelet made from them together with diamonds that I had purchased in Antwerp, but I wanted to wait until the timing was right, which it never was."

Kyla returned the gemstone to the box, closed the lid, said nothing. She handed it back to Matt.

Matt sensed the sudden change in her disposition. He returned the box to the drawer, put his arm around her. "You okay?" he said.

Kyla nodded. "It's nothing."

"It's obviously not nothing. Tell me."

Kyla sighed. "You and me, being at once in each other's lives and yet out of them. It feels... chaotic."

Matt nodded. "It does."

Kyla propped herself up. "Tell me something. And I want you to be completely honest with me."

"All right."

"If I could find a way for us to leave the agency, would you take it? Would you come with me?"

"In a heartbeat."

"Then that's what we should do."

"It's a romantic notion, Kyla. But it could never happen. The agency wouldn't permit it."

"What if they didn't know?"

"What are you talking about?"

"What if we gave them a reason to believe we were both dead?"

"What are you getting at?"

"I know someone who can help us. He owes me a favor. Actually, he owes me his life, so I'm pretty sure he'd come through no matter what I asked him to do for me."

"He's a facilitator?"

"One of the best in the business. He and his contacts can provide us with everything we'd need. Passports, new identities, even plastic surgery if we needed it."

"You're serious, aren't you?"

"More than I've been about anything in my life. If you really want for us to be together, I can make it happen."

"It sounds dangerous, Kyla."

"Like what we do now isn't?"

Matt nodded. "If the agency ever found out that we'd faked our own deaths..."

"They'd do what? Send someone to kill us? How is that any different from the situation we're in right now? You already have a capture/kill order issued against you, and the clock on that is running down every minute. If ever there was a time to do this, it's now."

"I don't know. I'll need time to think about it."

"Time is the one thing we don't have, Matt."

"If anything were to happen to you as a result of doing this, I'd never..."

"Nothing's going to happen to me."

"I can handle going down alone, but taking you down with me? That's a step too far."

"You're talking like the only end game here is one in which we both die."

"Because it's the most likely outcome."

"No, it isn't. To be honest, I've been thinking about it for quite some time."

"About us disappearing together?"

Kyla nodded. "I figured one day we'd find each other again. Don't ask me how. I just knew it. Call it intuition or whatever. I also knew that when that day finally came we'd have to act fast. That day is here. If you really want me, I'm here. Succeed or fail, we'll do it together. So, what's it going to be? Are we doing this, or what?"

Matt stared into Kyla's eyes, nodded. "We are."

Kyla smiled. "Good. I'll make the call in the morning. Right now, we both need a good night's sleep."

Matt rolled her onto her back. "Are you telling me you're tired?"

Kyla laughed. "I'm never *that* tired."

35

No Detours

FRANCESCA SLIPPED INTO her running shoes, put on a light jacket. Her grandmother stood beside her as she sat at the bottom of the stairs tying her shoelaces.

"Don't be long," Carla said. "Walk to the mission and see if your grandfather is there. If he's not, you're to come straight home. Got it?"

Francesca stood. "There and back," she replied. "Got it."

Carla shook her head. "I shouldn't have agreed to this. You're too young to be running around the streets at this hour."

Francesca leaned forward, kissed her grandmother on the cheek. "I'm sixteen, Gran," she said. "I'm not a little kid anymore. I can take care of myself."

"That's not what I'm worried about. It's the gangs. You

know what they're like. They come out at night, like vermin."

"I'll keep my distance," Francesca replied. "If anyone makes me feel uncomfortable, I'll cross the street."

"Do you have your pepper spray?"

Francesca retrieved the small canister from her jacket pocket, showed it to her grandmother.

"Good," Carla said. "Remember what your grandfather told you?"

"Don't think twice about using it if I have to."

"And then?"

"Run."

"Precisely."

Francesca wrapped her arms around her grandmother, hugged her. "You worry about me way too much."

Carla smiled. "You're my one and only granddaughter. Of course I'm going to worry about you. Consider yourself lucky. If your grandfather had his way, he'd pack you in bubble wrap every time you walked out the door."

Francesca laughed. "Thank goodness I have you to run interference for me."

"I'm serous, Francesca. You know this part of town has gotten more dangerous lately."

"So why don't we move?"

"Your grandfather and I have talked about it," Carla replied. "When you leave for university and are in a residence we'll look for a new place to live."

"Don't put off moving because of me, Gran. Never mind school. I'll be eligible to receive my learner's permit pretty soon. Once I get my driver's license, I won't need to rely on you or grandpa to chauffeur me around anymore."

"Your grandfather doesn't *chauffeur* you around, honey.

He drives you where you need to go because he wants to, not because he has to. It makes him feel good to do it."

Francesca opened the front door. "Regardless, I need to learn how to manage my life for myself. I can't have you and grandpa watching out for me 24/7."

Carla nodded. "You're right. You're not a little girl anymore."

"Definitely not," Francesca said. She removed the pepper spray from her pocket, dangled it on its keychain, winked. "Besides, I'm packing."

Carla laughed, kissed her goodbye as she stepped out the door. "To the mission and back. No detours. Got it?"

"Got it."

"I expect to see you back here in thirty minutes."

"All right."

"That means no dillydallying."

"Enough, already!" Francesca called out as she walked down the steps and onto the sidewalk. "I'll be fine."

Carla watched her granddaughter walk up the street until she was out of sight, then closed and locked the door.

She checked her watch. Domenic had been gone for well over an hour now.

"Something isn't right," she said aloud. "Something just isn't right."

36

AREA 1

THE NAVIGATOR SLOWED to a stop. The driver opened his door and exited the vehicle while Forsythe and his bodyguards waited in the car with Domenic.

"Where are we?" Domenic asked.

The men said nothing.

Domenic watched through the front window of the SUV as the driver unlocked a padlock hanging between two anchor posts, unwound the length of steel chain which joined them, and let it fall to the ground. He read the sign affixed to the gate: **FUTURE HOME OF FOREST HILL TOWERS. DANGER: CONSTRUCTION ZONE. NO UNAUTHORIZED PERSONS BEYOND THIS POINT.** The driver rolled the gate aside wide enough to allow the SUV to enter. Ahead, the vehicle's headlights illuminated the pitch-black site.

The driver returned to the car, proceeded through the gate.

"Take us to Area 1," Forsythe demanded.

"Yes, sir," the driver replied.

"What's Area 1?" Domenic asked. "What are we doing here?"

The bodyguard seated beside Domenic spoke. "You ask a lot of questions, don't you?"

Domenic tried to maintain his composure. "Whatever you're planning on doing to me you're wasting your time. I have the mayor on speed dial. One call to him and—"

"That reminds me," Forsythe said. "Give me your phone."

"I don't have it with me," Domenic replied.

"Please, Mr. Vitagliano," the drug lord said. "Don't play with me. That would be an insult to my intelligence and yours." He held out his hand. "Your phone, please. Now."

Domenic opened his jacket, removed his cell phone.

"Thank you," Forsythe said. "Please hand it to my associate."

Domenic did as he was told. The bodyguard slipped the phone into his coat pocket, then elbowed Domenic in his ribs. "The next time Mr. Forsythe asks you to do something, do it."

"That's enough," Forsythe said. He glanced at Domenic. "Are you all right, Mr. Vitagliano?"

Domenic recovered from the sudden blow, let out a long, slow breath. "I'm sixty-eight years old," he replied. "What do you think?"

"I *think* that by now you would have learned to think before you speak."

"Normally, I do. But whenever I'm in the company of an asshole, my inner voice has a habit of becoming my outer voice. It's an age thing. You'll understand that one day, assuming that you get to live as long as I have. Which I seriously doubt will be the case."

"Oh?" Forsythe said. "Why is that?"

"Because hell has a special place for people like you. And my guess is Satan's going to come for you a lot sooner than you think."

Forsythe smiled. "He and I have been on good terms for many years. I'm not the least bit worried about that."

"You should be."

The SUV slowed to a stop. The driver placed the vehicle in Park.

"It seems we have arrived," Forsythe said. "Come, Mr. Vitagliano. There's something I want you to see."

Domenic remained seated as Forsythe exited the vehicle. "I'm not going anywhere," he said.

Forsythe peered into the car, nodded to his bodyguard. The man grabbed Domenic by his arm, pulled him out. Domenic fell to the ground.

"On your feet," the bodyguard ordered.

Domenic grabbed the door handle, held onto it for support, pulled himself to his feet. He stared at the bodyguard. "I really wish I was your age," he said.

The bodyguard smiled. "Why's that?"

"Because I'd clean your goddamn clock."

The bodyguard shook his head. "I've got to give it to you, old man," he said. "You've got a pair on you."

"You have no idea," Domenic replied.

"Problem is, you're all bark and no bite."

"You want to find out how much bite I've got?" Domenic stood tall, let go of the door handle, took a step back, raised his fists. "Come on, numbnuts. Try me."

Forsythe's second bodyguard stepped out of the SUV, grabbed Domenic by his arms, held him in place.

Domenic struggled, glanced over his shoulder at the man holding him, then back at his antagonist. "Figures a wimp like you would need backup," he said.

The bodyguard stepped toward Domenic. "You're really beginning to piss me off," he said.

"Enough," Forsythe said. "Let him go."

The two men stood down, released him.

Forsythe motioned to Domenic. "Please, come with me."

Domenic followed behind the drug lord. "Where are we going?" he asked.

"You'll see."

The two men walked through the construction site. Forsythe's bodyguards followed.

"This project has been in development for a year," Forsythe said. "It used to be a garment factory. Now only a few walls remain. Soon it will be a twenty-story condominium tower housing two-hundred-and-forty residential units."

"Is that supposed to impress me?" Domenic asked.

"I don't care if you're impressed or not," Forsythe replied. "It merely leads me to my point."

"Which is?"

"That everything has a lifespan, Mr. Vitagliano. Buildings, people... it's all the same. Over time, it becomes necessary to replace the old with the new, the aged with the young. Our society calls that progress. I call it opportunity."

"Meaning?"

"Wait here. I'll show you."

Forsythe walked twenty feet ahead, removed an item from his jacket pocket, slipped it into a crack in a concrete wall, then returned to where he had been standing.

"I'm sure that by now you've concluded that the fire which destroyed the Guiding Light Mission was no accident. I needed that plaza, and you were the last remaining hold-out. Now that the property is free and clear, I'll be able to proceed with my plans to develop it as I see fit."

"Good luck with that," Domenic replied. "The fire marshal's office will conclude it was arson."

Forsythe nodded. "Yes, they will. Because you are going to tell them that it was you who started the blaze."

Domenic stared at the drug dealer. "You must be out of your mind. I would never admit to doing something like that."

"Oh, I think you would. Given the proper motivation, of course."

"What are you talking about?"

Forsythe pointed to the wall. "Perhaps you should take a closer look at that wall."

Domenic stared at the concrete wall, said nothing.

Forsythe pointed. "Now, Mr. Vitagliano."

Domenic walked to the wall, paused.

Forsythe called out. "You see what I mean?"

Domenic plucked out the photo Forsythe had placed in the wall's crack. It was a picture of Francesca, taken from a distance using a telephoto lens. He turned, looked back at the drug dealer.

In his hand, Forsythe held a control box. "I would

suggest you move to your left, Mr. Vitagliano," he said. "Quickly."

Domenic heard a strange sound in front of him, like the uncoupling of a heavy metal object from its anchoring mechanism. He stepped aside as a three-foot wide steel wrecking ball came hurtling toward him out of the darkness. It broke through the concrete wall at the very spot where he had been standing.

"Jesus!" he called out.

Forsythe's tone turned cold. "Let me tell you what you are going to do next, Mr. Vitagliano. Tomorrow, you're going to walk into Police Precinct 43 in The Bronx and tell the desk sergeant that you wish to make a confession, and that it was you who started the fire at the mission. Give them whatever reason you want. I don't care what it is."

"And if I refuse?"

"Then my associates will reset the wrecking ball, replace the picture you are holding with Francesca, and end your granddaughter's life in a most horrific way."

Domenic stared at the deadly steel ball, watched it sway back and forth. Dear god, he thought. Not Francesca. "If I do what you ask you'll leave my family alone?" he asked.

"You have my word."

"That means nothing to me."

"Be that as it may, it's all you're going to get."

Domenic nodded. "All right," he said. "I'll do it. Just don't hurt Francesca."

"A wise decision," Forsythe replied. "Now, what do you say we get you back home? I'm sure your wife and granddaughter are wondering where you've gotten to."

Domenic accompanied the four men back to the Navigator. He said nothing on the return trip to the mission. His thoughts kept rushing back to the image of the wrecking ball, and Francesca.

When they arrived back at the mission, the drug lord instructed his bodyguard to return Domenic's cell phone to him as he stepped out of the SUV.

Forsythe lowered the window. "Tomorrow, Mr. Vitagliano," he said. "We'll be waiting."

Domenic watched the Navigator drive off. As he turned to walk home, Francesca rounded the corner.

She saw him, smiled, and waved.

Domenic waved back, then felt his heart slam in his chest.

37

Two At The Most

THE FOLLOWING MORNING Kyla awoke to find Matt standing in front of the full-length mirror in his bedroom, fully dressed. She wiped the sleep from her eyes, retrieved her phone from the bedside table next to her, checked the time. It was 8:30 A.M.

"I hope you weren't planning on leaving without saying goodbye," she said.

Matt tucked his pistol into the small of his back, glanced at her in the mirror. "Of course not," he said. "But you were so out of it I didn't want to disturb you."

"Was I snoring?"

Matt smiled. "Maybe a little."

"Oh, god," Kyla said. She pulled the pillow out from under her head, pressed it over her face, talked into it. "How embarrassing!"

"It's nothing to be embarrassed about."

Kyla moved the pillow aside, peeked out at Matt. "Loudly?"

Matt held his smile, said nothing.

Mortified, Kyla pressed the pillow back down over her head. "I was! Oh Lord, kill me now!"

Matt chuckled. "I kind of liked it."

"I know what I sound like when I snore. A jet fighter taking off from an aircraft carrier makes less noise than I do."

Matt smiled. "No comment."

Kyla pulled the covers over her head.

Matt laughed, walked to her side of the bed, pulled back the covers, kissed her forehead. "I have to go out for a while. The fridge is stocked. Help yourself to whatever you want. There's a Keurig on the counter and a box of coffee pods beside it."

"Where are you going?"

"To find Benny Ortiz."

"The kid whose phone you ran through Unicorn?"

"Yeah."

"You want company?"

Matt shook his head. "This will be a conversation best had one-on-one."

"You expect him to give you trouble?"

"Probably."

"But you said he's just a kid."

"A kid who likes to play with knives."

"He's ganged up?"

"Unfortunately, yes."

Kyla sat up. "You sure you don't need me to back you up?"

"I'll be fine. It's nothing I can't handle on my own."

"I don't know, Matt. I have a bad feeling about this."

"About what?"

"You making yourself so visible."

"No one knows I'm here except for you. I know how to stay off the radar."

"Let's hope it stays that way."

"Meaning?"

"Remember who we report to. Ferriman can't be trusted."

"Which is why you're going to shower, have breakfast, then call your contact and get the wheels in motion to get us out of here."

"He's a facilitator, Matt, not a magician. He'll need time to prepare our documents and passports."

"You said he owes you a favor, right?"

"Yes."

"Then call him on it. Tell him it's urgent and that you need him to expedite the process."

Kyla nodded. "How much time will you need to do what you have to do?"

"A day, two at the most."

"Any particular place you want him to send us?"

"Honduras. I want to finish the Gutierrez assignment. But I'm going to do it on my terms, not Ferriman's."

Kyla nodded. "That would be perfect. I know people in Honduras who can help us, plus you can clear your name with the agency. We can kill two birds with one stone."

"If that's possible," Matt said. He left the bedroom.

Kyla called out after him. "Matt?"

Matt turned, looked back. "Yeah?"

"Be careful."

"Always."

38

Gone

DOMENIC SAID LITTLE after he and Francesca arrived home the previous night. Carla knew better than to press him for answers when he was in this frame of mind. She had seen it many times over the years. The pressures of running the restaurant. The challenges of establishing and building the Guiding Light Mission. And worst of all, how inside of himself he had withdrawn after the death of their son and daughter-in-law. She probed lightly. "You got in late. I was expecting you sooner. How was your walk?"

Domenic sat at the kitchen table stirring his coffee. He removed the spoon, set it on the napkin beside his plate, stared at the cup, watched the hot liquid swirl. "All right," he answered.

Carla continued. "Francesca said she found you at the mission."

Domenic brought the cup to his lips, took a sip, nodded.

"Are you sure it's a good idea to go back there right now?"

Domenic looked up. "Why wouldn't it be?"

Carla sensed the tension in his voice. "Perhaps the fire marshal's office would prefer it if people stayed away from the scene."

"I'm not just *any* people. It was my place. If I want to camp out there, I will."

"I'm just saying…"

"Don't press me on this, Carla."

"I'm not."

"Yes, you are!"

Domenic picked up his coffee mug, left the room.

"Your breakfast is almost ready," Carla called out after him. "Just another few min—"

Domenic barked his response. "I'm not hungry."

Francesca entered the kitchen as her grandfather stormed past her. "Whoa," she said, sidestepping him. She stared at her grandmother. "What eating Grandpa?"

Carla shook her head. "He's just upset about the fire." She set a plate on the table for her granddaughter.

Francesca dropped her backpack at her feet, took a seat, poured herself a glass of orange juice. "Tell me about it. He didn't say two words to me during our walk home last night."

"Your grandfather has always had a hard time dealing with tragedy," Carla replied. "Give him time. He'll come around."

Francesca nodded. "I get it," she said. "He put his heart and soul into the mission. We all did."

"But it was your grandfather's dream," Carla said. She lifted a generous helping of scrambled eggs out of the frying pan and set them on Francesca's plate, together with three strips of bacon. "There's a difference."

"I know." Francesca replied. She paused. "Are you sure I shouldn't stay home today? I really think grandpa needs to talk. And you know how good I can be at drawing the truth out of him."

Carla smiled. "You have him wrapped around your little finger, don't you?"

Francesca picked up a slice of crispy bacon, took a bite. "Maybe. But the fact is he knows he can talk to me about anything."

"Be that as it may, I know your grandfather better than you do. And right now, what he needs most of all is space."

Francesca nodded. "Fair enough."

Carla glanced at the kitchen clock. "Eat up, young lady," she said. "You're running late."

Francesca shoveled the remaining bacon strips and several forkfuls of egg into her mouth, washed it down with orange juice. "I know, I know." She wiped her mouth, crumpled the napkin, set it on the table, rose from her chair, snatched her backpack from the floor. "I'm outa here."

"Excuse me," Carla said. "Aren't you forgetting something?" She tapped her cheek with her finger.

Francesca smiled, ran to her grandmother, kissed her on the cheek, then darted out of the room.

"That's better," Carla said. "Don't forget to kiss your grandfather goodbye, too."

Francesca's voice echoed through the main hallway. "I won't!"

Domenic stood in his main floor study, staring out the window.

Francesca entered the room, ran to him. "Bye, Grandpa," she said.

Domenic smiled, hugged her. "Goodbye, sweetheart." He kissed her forehead. "Have a good day at school."

"I will." Francesca paused. "Grandpa, will you do me a favor?"

"What?"

"Try not to let this whole situation with the mission get to you too much. Grandma's just as upset about it as you are. It hurts her when you get mad like this. All she wants to do is help, so let her."

Domenic stared down at his granddaughter, smiled. "You're far wiser than your years, you know that?"

Francesca smiled. "Yes, I am. And don't you forget it."

Domenic laughed. "I won't."

"Good. Now go have breakfast with Grandma before it gets cold."

"Yes, ma'am."

Francesca opened the front door, bounded down the stairs, waved goodbye.

Domenic waved back, then turned his attention back to the street. The white SUV he had been observing from the window in his study slowly pulled away from the curb.

An unsettling feeling came over him. He remembered Forsythe's threat from last night. He watched the car accelerate up the road, pass Francesca, brake to a sudden stop, then speed away.

In a split-second, his granddaughter was gone.

39

So Many Moving Parts

KYLA HEARD HER phone ring as she stepped out of the shower. She wrapped herself in a towel, ran into the bedroom, retrieved it from the nightstand, read the name on the screen: FERRIMAN.

She listened to the brief message the CIA director left on her voicemail. "Where are you, Reese?" Ferriman had said. "I need a sitrep on Reaper. Call me the second you get this message."

Kyla thought about what she would say in her situation report to her director. She needed to buy time. Ferriman wasn't the type to accept excuses. The report she provided would have to be viable enough to prevent him from stepping up the timetable he had given her. She knew him well enough to know that often what he said and did were two different things. She paced Matt's bedroom, formulated a response. Several thoughts raced through her mind. Did she still have operational exclusivity, or had the order been opened to the field, the net for Matt cast far and wide? Had a team of assets been deployed? If so, were they already in Soundview, watching them both, waiting for the right moment to take out Matt? Had she been followed? There were so many moving parts to the equation, everything so unpredictable. There was only one thing she could do. It was a career-ending move, but so be it. They had already agreed to leave the country. With any luck, Matt would only require today to conclude his business with Benny Ortiz and help the family with whom he had become so close so fast.

She would have to lie to Ferriman.

She was aware of the consequences that such an action would bring if that truth was revealed. She too would be classified as an Alpha Priority One target. Ferriman would issue an order. They would be eliminated on sight. One thing was certain. Whatever she said in the next few minutes would decide their fate. They would live or face death. The only remaining question was how long it would be before they found themselves facing down their executioner. Ferriman would send his next best asset. Worst-case scenario, he would pull out all the stops and send a team, which would only make matters worse. After she completed the call, she would contact her contact, the facilitator. Their plan to escape couldn't wait any longer. They would have to leave tonight, regardless of whether Matt had concluded his business on behalf of the family or not. Their very lives depended on them getting as far away from the United States as they could, the faster the better.

Kyla took a deep breath, calmed herself, placed the call.

"Ferriman."

"It's Reese, sir."

The director's response was cold. "Where the hell were you?"

"I'm sorry, sir. I was away from my phone."

"Where are you with Reaper?"

She lied. "Still trying to locate him, sir."

"What are you doing in The Bronx?"

Kyla remembered her phone was being tracked. "Following a lead."

"Is it solid?"

"I'll know later today."

"You're in Soundview."

"Yes, sir."

"Why there?"

"Sir?"

"You could have gone anywhere, but you went there first. Why?"

Kyla paused. "It was something Gamble told me once."

"And that is?"

"He likes it here. Nothing more complicated than that, sir."

"We're talking about an operative who has travelled the world undertaking missions for his country,"

Ferriman said. "Yet when he goes rogue, he selects a tiny borough in New York City?"

"It's the best lead I have, sir."

"Doesn't sound like much of a lead at all."

"I don't follow."

"It sounds like you took a direct route. Like you already knew where he would be."

"I assure you that's not the case, sir."

"Then you won't mind if I send someone to help you."

"That won't be necessary."

Ferriman ignored her objection. "I'm narrowing your window. You'll have until the end of the day to find Gamble. No later."

Kyla felt her heart jump. "I understand, sir."

"Check into the Bronx safe house with Reaper tonight, then await further instructions. I expect to see you both here at Langley tomorrow."

"Yes, sir."

"I gave you this assignment because you convinced me you were up to the task, Reese. Don't make me believe I made a mistake in doing so."

"You haven't, sir."

"The safe house. Midnight tonight."

"Yes, sir."

Ferriman terminated the call.

Kyla felt her stomach drop. She knew what that meant. Ferriman had no intention of waiting for the proverbial midnight strike of the bell. The second he had hung up the phone with her he'd made another call. A local asset had been mobilized. If she was to put distance between them and the assassin, she would have to act fast.

In addition to the agency accessing borough-wide CCTV and police observation device cameras, the asset's first directive would be to track her phone.

Outside, Kyla heard the distant sound of a city sanitation truck rounding the corner to begin its garbage collection on the street outside Matt's townhouse.

She dressed quickly, ran to the door, walked down the front steps, then deposited her cellphone in a neighbor's trash can.

She returned to Matt's townhouse, peered through the small window in the front door, watched as the garbage truck picked up the can, deposited its contents into its tailgate, then continued on its way.

It was a long shot. The phone could be crushed by its compactor in the collection process and destroyed, or not. Kyla prayed for the latter to be the case.

The truck continued on its route up the street. She hoped her plan would work. As long as the phone remained operational, its signal would continue to transmit, which would show her in motion. The asset would follow the signal first, try to locate her. Right now, the one thing she needed most of all was to buy time. This was a good start.

She had noticed a bodega around the corner from Matt's townhouse. Like every convenience store in New York City, it would sell disposable cellphones, 'burners' as they were called on the street. She would purchase one, call Matt, reiterate her conversation with Ferriman. He needed to know the danger to them was imminent, and that their time in New York City was up.

They had no choice now. They had to be out of the country by tonight.

Kyla ran upstairs, grabbed her gun off the bedside table, slipped it into her waistband, then left the townhouse for the bodega.

After purchasing the burner phone and calling Matt, there would be one call left to make; one that would mean the difference between life and death. She would reach out to Oleg Schroeder, also known as the Facilitator, and enlist his help to get them out of the country before midnight. If he couldn't, it would be over for them both.

She recognized the tone of Ferriman's voice when in the

past when he'd ordered her to end the lives of former rogue operators.

They needed to move fast.

If they didn't, they would be dead by morning.

40

Sweet Pea

FORSYTHE'S CELL PHONE rang. He answered the call. "Yes?"

"We have her, sir," Glenn said.

"Did she give you any trouble?"

"She landed a punch on my busted cheek," the enforcer replied. "No big deal."

"Where are you now?"

"En route to the Forest Hill Towers site."

"All right. Wait until I get there. In the meantime, keep her quiet and out of sight."

In the backseat of the Navigator, Francesca stirred, then moaned.

"Was that her I just heard?" Forsythe asked.

"Yeah. She's coming around now."

"What do you mean, coming around?"

"She started kicking, punching, and biting. I had to rag her."

"You *chloroformed* her?"

"Had to. Bitch was out of control."

"What the fuck is the matter with you? You couldn't control a sixteen-year-old teenager without rendering her unconscious?"

"She was causing a problem."

"What kind of problem? Did she have a knife to your throat?"

"No."

"A gun in your face?"

"No."

"Then she must have shoved a fucking bazooka down your throat. That's it, right? A bazooka?"

"No, sir," Glenn said sheepishly. "No knife. No gun. No bazooka."

"No weapon of any kind?"

"No."

"Just her hands and feet?"

"And teeth."

"Oh, right. Her teeth. I'll bet you were terrified that she was going to chew you to death."

"No, sir. I wasn't."

"Yet you saw fit to expose her to a highly toxic drug."

"With all due respect, sir, what's the big deal?"

"Did you check her wrist?"

"Her wrist?"

"Yes, her wrist. The bracelet she's wearing. Flip it over. Read what it says on the back."

Francesca cowered as Glenn leaned in beside her, grabbed her wrist, pulled up her jacket sleeve, found the braided blue paracord medical band, turned over the silver disc affixed to it, read the inscription aloud: "FRANCESCA VITAGLIANO, ASTHMA."

"That's right, you idiot," Forsythe said. "She has asthma. Everyone who knows the family knows that. Old man Vitagliano organizes a fundraiser every year for the American Lung Association on her behalf. You're lucky the chloroform didn't shut down her respiratory system and kill her on the spot."

Glenn had had enough of his boss's condescending attitude, became defensive. "So what if it did?" he said. "We both know she's not leaving the construction site in one piece."

Forsythe was furious. He forced himself to maintain his composure, took a deep breath, chose his words carefully. "Now you listen to me and listen good. No harm is to come to that girl. None whatsoever. When I arrive I don't want to find a single mark on her body or a strand of hair out of place. If I do, it won't be her that will be staring down the wrecking ball. It will be you. She has value to me because she provides me with leverage. Vitagliano will do anything I ask him to do if it means getting his precious granddaughter back alive and well and in one piece. On the other hand, your value to me is determined solely by your ability to follow orders. That's it. You're not paid to think or make decisions. Do I make myself clear?"

Glenn glared at Francesca. The teen held his stare. The enforcer twisted her wrist as he answered. "Yes, sir."

Francesca fought the pain, tightened her lips, grimaced.

"Good. Now tell me about Vitagliano."

"What about him?"

"Did he leave his house before you picked up the girl?"

"No."

"That son of a bitch. I gave him specific instructions. He should have left by now to turn himself into the cops."

"You want me to put a team on the house? Tell them to keep an eye on him?"

"No. I have a better idea. Something more motivating."

"What's that?"

"Take off her bracelet."

Francesca cried out as Glenn grabbed her arm and forcibly removed the medical device. "Got it," he said.

"Take her to the construction site, then go back to the house. Give the old man the bracelet. Tell him if he wants to see his granddaughter again to do what I told him to do. Assure him that if he doesn't the bracelet will be the last he ever sees of her."

"Understood."

"Call me when it's done."

"Yes, sir."

Forsythe ended the call.

Glenn placed his cell phone in his jacket pocket, stared at the teen, put his hand on her leg, massaged her thigh. He smiled. "I'll bet that sweet ass of yours has rocked a few worlds, hasn't it?" he asked.

Francesca tried to pull away, couldn't. The back seat of the car offered no escape from Glenn's advances.

"Take your hand off my leg," she warned.

"Or what?"

"Or I'll fucking kill you."

Glenn laughed, turned to his colleagues, called out. "When was the last time either of you fine gentlemen had some Grade A Number 1 high school tail?"

Evans drove while Darnell Edwards rode shotgun beside him in the front seat and nursed his broken arm.

Darnell answered. "If you know what's good for you, you'll put that thought out of your mind right now."

"Why?" Glenn replied. "You gonna say something?"

"No."

"What about you, Evans?"

Evans shook his head. "Don't drag me into your shit," he said. "It's your funeral, not mine."

"Then we understand each other," Glenn replied. He turned to Francesca and smiled. "We understand each other, too. Don't we, Sweet Pea?"

A tear formed in Francesca's eye, rolled down her cheek.

Glenn wiped it away. "Yeah," he said. "We sure do."

41

One Simple Question

MATT REACHED THE intersection where he had previously run into Benny Ortiz, crossed the street, kept his eyes open for the kid. From the conversation he had overheard last night and the information he had been able to retrieve from his phone, he knew the kid was associated with David Forsythe and the Diamondback gang. This was the third run-in he had had with members of Forsythe's crew. The first had been in the Guiding Light Mission where he had relieved one of the three members of his weapon and severely injured them all. The second was the incident involving the young punk who had tried to mug the elderly couple at knifepoint and received a broken wrist for his trouble. Benny Ortiz had been his most recent encounter. It sickened Matt to know how deeply the gang had penetrated the part of the Bronx he loved so much. He remembered what Kyla had said to him, how time was running out, and that they had to get out of New York and the country as soon as possible. But that was not going to happen until he had excised the cancer that was the Diamondbacks from the streets of Soundview and left the area as he had found it so many years ago; quiet, unassuming, friendly, and peaceful. From the sound of the conversation he had overheard, Benny Ortiz was closely connected to Forsythe. He needed to know everything he knew about the gang and how to take them down.

Two blocks from the intersection, Matt reached a corner. He stopped, looked around, observed the area, recognized one of the buildings from the large **B** on its wall. It was Block B, the same building Domenic had told him Angelina Ruffalo lived with her disabled daughter, Cassidy. A group of young men stood on the sidewalk in front of the twenty-story tower. They eyed Matt as he approached them, then began to walk in his direction. They stopped several feet in front of him.

The leader of the group spoke. "You lost or something?"

Matt shook his head. "Just out for a stroll," he answered. "How are you boys doing this morning?"

"This ain't no place for a stroll," the leader replied. "You need to turn around and go back to whatever latte sipping part of town you came from."

Matt smiled. "Actually, I'm not a latte guy. I'll have a peppermint mocha or a caramel macchiato every once in a while, but black is more my style."

The leader got in Matt's face. "Do I look like a fucking barista to you? Bounce, bitch!"

Matt eyed the men as they surrounded him. "You boys

sure you want to do this?" he asked. "It's a little early in the morning for getting your asses kicked, don't you think?"

"Last chance," the leader said. "Leave."

Matt stared into his eyes. "And if I choose not to?"

The leader pulled a knife from his hip pocket, pressed a button on its barrel. The four-inch blade shot out of the handgrip of the weapon, locked into place. "Then I'm gonna have to carve you up."

"I'd prefer you didn't," Matt replied. "This is my favorite jacket."

The man positioned the tip of his blade over Matt's heart, pressed gently. "I'm gonna enjoy this," he said.

Matt stared down at the knife, felt its sharp tip break his skin, heard more clicks as the men around him readied their blades. "Final warning," he said. "Put them away now, or you'll wear them."

The leader smiled. "I don't think s—"

Matt made his move. He stepped back, distanced himself from his would-be attacker, kicked out at the man behind him. The blade of his foot connected with the thug's kneecap. The man screamed as his leg folded inward at a horrific angle, his kneecap clearly broken. Unable to support his weight, he dropped to the ground. Matt's training took over. He dropped low, stayed in motion, swept out the leg of the attacker on his right, watched the man fall, heard his head smack the ground with a sickening crack, then sprang to his feet and faced the leader. The man rushed him, sliced at the air madly with his switchblade. Matt waited for the right moment, caught the thug's wrist, turned it back on him, stepped forward, and thrust the knife down violently. The blade followed the trajectory of Matt's rapid defensive move and buried itself deep into the man's shoulder. Matt held on to the leader, waited until his last two attackers charged him, then pulled the blade out of the man, hauled him to his feet, and pressed it against his throat.

The men stopped in their tracks.

"You two really want to be responsible for this asshole breathing through a tube for the rest of his life?" Matt warned. "Because that's what the street's going to say. Don't believe me? Look around."

The men stared at the crowd that had gathered in the driveway of Building B to watch the fight. Above them, residents stared down from their balconies, cell phones in hand, all pointed in their direction.

"My guess is at least twenty people are filming us right now," Matt said. "What do you think the odds are of at least one person making sure their footage gets to Forsythe?"

At the mention of David Forsythe's name, the men relaxed. Their desire to come to the rescue of their leader left them.

"Retract the knives. Throw them over here."

Their leader struggled to free himself from Matt's firm hold. "Do that and you're fucking dead," he yelled to his men. "You hear me? Fucking dead!"

The men ignored their boss's command, secured the weapons, tossed their knives at Matt's feet. "Smart move," Matt said. "Now tell me where I can find Benny Ortiz."

The men said nothing.

"Really?" Matt said. "That's how you're gonna play this?"

The man who had suffered a broken knee spoke. He pushed himself up onto his elbow, pointed down the road. "Ortiz is in Building C," he grunted.

"Which apartment?" Matt asked.

"Main floor. 118."

Matt spoke to the leader while keeping a sharp eye on the men. "All of this could have been avoided if you'd just answered one simple question. Now you're going to have to explain to Forsythe how you and members of your crew got fucked up. My guess is that when you do there will be repercussions. It's a pretty safe assumption that your days of running with the Diamondbacks are over. If I were you, I'd make one last move while you still can."

The blade of his own knife still pressed firmly against his throat, the leader spoke. "What's that?"

Matt released him, pushed him forward.

The thug stumbled, regained his footing, then turned and faced Matt.

"Get the hell out of Soundview," Matt said. He pulled his gun from his waistband for them to see, held it at his side. "For the record, that's not a request. You're done here. Now pick up your friend and leave. If I see any of you again I'll drop you on sight. We clear?"

The men stared at their leader, waited for him to respond to Matt's threat. He didn't.

"One last thing," Matt said.

"What's that?" the leader asked.

"When you see Forsythe later, which I know you will, give him a message."

"What's that?"

"Tell him Reaper is coming for him."

42

Deal

MATT WATCHED THE men walk away. He collected their weapons from the ground, shoved the switchblades into his back pocket. The crowd that had been filming the action had lost interest, dispersed. He slipped his gun back into his waistband, turned, then walked down the street to Building C where he had been told he could find Benny Ortiz.

Building C was a carbon copy of Building B, as were the two additional low-income high-rise apartment towers on the block, A and D. He entered the main floor lobby and walked down the corridor until he reached apartment 118, knocked on the door, waited for a response. None came. He pressed his ear to the door, heard movement inside. He knocked a second time.

"Who is it?" a voice called out. It belonged to an elderly woman.

"City inspector," Matt lied.

"Just a moment, please."

Matt heard the rattling of the security chain against the door as it was unhooked, followed by the disengaging of three deadbolts. The door creaked open. An old woman held onto the handgrips of her walker. She looked up at Matt, offered a smile. "Hello, dear," she said. "Can I help you?"

A second voice emanated from somewhere inside the small apartment. It belonged to a teenager. "Did you call me, Gran?"

"No, sweetie," the kindly old lady replied. "I was talking to this young man. He says he's with the city."

The teen entered the room. "Gran, what did I tell you about opening the door to strangers?" He looked at Matt, recognized him immediately. "You're the guy from last night," he said. "What the fuck are you doing here?"

"Benjamin Carlos Ortiz!" his grandmother said. "What have I told you about using foul language in this home?"

Matt watched Benny's hand dart to his back pocket. He knew he was going for his knife, likely the same one he had threatened him with last night. Matt stared at the young thug, warned him with his eyes. *Don't do it. Not here, and especially not in front of your grandmother.*

The kid understood. He gave Matt a menacing look, then turned his attention back to his grandmother. "It's okay, Gran," he said. "Go back and watch your show. I'll take care of this."

"Are you sure?"

"Yes."

"Well, alrighty then." The old lady smiled at Matt. "It was nice to meet you."

Matt nodded. "Same here, ma'am."

Benny turned his grandmother around, pointed her in the direction of the living room. "I'll be there in a few minutes," he said.

"All right, dear," she replied. After a few steps, the woman shuffled to a stop. "Don't forget to make our guest a nice cup of tea."

"I won't, Gran."

After another step. "And there are cookies in the cupboard."

"Yes, Gran," Benny replied as he stared into Matt's eyes, keeping the tone of his voice controlled, trying not to lose patience with his grandmother. "Tea and cookies. Got it."

When his grandmother finally left the narrow corridor and rounded the corner into the living room, Benny turned on Matt. "What the fuck are you doing here?"

Matt removed the kid's phone from his pocket, held it up.

"That's mine!" Benny exclaimed. "I've been looking everywhere for it. How did you—?"

"Doesn't matter," Matt interrupted. "What matters is what you know. And you're going to tell me everything."

"Know? About what?"

"David Forsythe, for starters. And the fire at the Guiding Light Mission."

Benny tried to slam the door. Matt blocked it with his foot, kept it open, forced his way inside, pulled his gun, pressed it against the kid's forehead. "This can go one of two ways," Matt whispered. "Easy or hard. I'm good with either. Choose."

Benny began to tremble. "Easy."

"That what I thought you'd say."

"Don't hurt me," Benny pleaded. "I take care of my gran. I'm all she's got."

"I'm not here to hurt you, but I will if I have to. Got it?"

The teen nodded.

"Where's your room?"

Benny motioned down the hall.

"Anyone else here?"

"No."

"Good. Now move." Matt followed the teen down the hallway, entered his room behind him, closed the door.

Benny sat on his bed while Matt took a seat in the kid's computer desk chair. "You never answered my question," he said. "Who are you?"

"Consider me a concerned citizen."

"Bad for you, then."

"How's that?"

"Every *citizen* around here knows better than to ask questions about David Forsythe, and they especially know not to ask about his business."

"I guess that makes me the exception to the rule."

"No, that makes you a fucking idiot. You must be anxious to make the news as the East River's floater of the week."

Matt took out the kid's phone, placed it on his computer desk. "You want this back or not?"

"Yeah, I want it back. My whole fucking life is in there."

Matt nodded. "I know."

"You broke into my phone? How did you—"

"I'm the nosey type. Enough with the drama, Benjamin. Start talking."

"It's *Benny*."

"Whatever."

"I can't."

"Can't, or won't?"

"Won't."

"Why not?"

"He'll kill me, that's why."

"You mean Forsythe?"

Benny nodded. "Then he'll kill my gran."

"No, he won't."

"How do you know?"

"Because I plan to kill him myself."

The teen leaned back. "You a pro or something?"

"Or something."

"No shit." Benny stared at Matt, sized him up. "If I talk, what's to stop you from killing me and my gran after I tell you what you want to know about Forsythe?"

"I have standards. Not killing my informants is one of them."

"You'd be the first."

"The Guiding Light Mission. It was professionally torched, wasn't it?"

"What makes you think I'd know anything about that?"

Matt held up the phone.

"Oh, yeah. My bad."

"Who did it?"

"Some dude out of Boston. He flew in a few days ago."

"This dude have a name?"

"They call him Mr. Wick, as in light the wick and wait for the fire."

"How original."

"Hey, you asked."

"Is he still here?"

"Wick?" Benny shrugged. "No clue."

"Why does Forsythe want the mission so badly?"

"It's not just the mission he wants. It's the whole fucking block."

"Why?"

Benny paused. "You've gone through my phone, right?"

"Answer the question."

"Because he's outgrown his current meth production facility. Dude can't make enough of that shit to meet the demand."

"You're talking about Sapphire Slam?"

"Yeah. He plans to build a condo tower where the mission is now, one with a secret sub-basement, then set up a super lab in there. It'll take a couple of years to complete, but when it's finished the lab will take up the entire block. It'll be fucking epic."

"Where is his lab located now?"

"In the basement of Red Thunder."

"What's that?"

"A fireworks manufacturing company in Hunt's Point. It's on the water, a block from the fish market. The location's perfect. He ships Slam up and down the East River and upstate to Connecticut. Like it or not, you gotta hand it to the guy. He's a fucking genius."

"No, he's a criminal and a sociopath."

"That's your opinion."

"Sounds like someone needs a better role model."

Benny laughed. "Role model? You serious? Look around you, man. You see where I live. I hate to break it to you, but role models are in short fucking supply in this neighborhood. My old man checked in to Rikers when I was fourteen. He's doing life on a murder rap. I never knew my mom, just my gran. I'm too short to play pro sports and I can't carry a tune to save my life. That leaves the street. This here's the jungle, and I'm on my own. It's all about survival, man. You wanna eat and not get the shit beaten out of you every day? No problem. Strap up and play the game. That's it. There are no fairy tale endings around here, brother. It's one day at a time until you die."

Matt had all the information he needed. He stood, handed Benny his cell phone. "You want to make a better life for you and your grandmother?"

Benny stared at Matt suspiciously. "And how the hell am I supposed to do that?"

"Give me a few hours and you'll see. But I'm going to need something from you in return."

"I figured there was a catch. There always is."

Matt shook his head. "No catch."

"What then?"

"Your silence."

"Meaning?"

"The second I leave this apartment you're going to want to phone Forsythe and try to make points with him by telling him about me and filling him in on our conversation. That would be a mistake."

"Or not."

"Trust me, it would."

Benny crossed his arms. "How do I know you're not going to fuck me over?"

"Because I won't. I have a plan, but I'll need time to execute it. If it goes the way I expect it will, I'll be back in touch soon."

"And if you're not?"

"Then I'll probably be dead." Matt extended his hand. "What do you say? Do we have a deal?"

Benny paused, then reached out, shook it. "Yeah."

"One last question," Matt said.

"What?"

"Why did you tell me what you know about Forsythe and his operation?"

"You mean aside from the fact you had a gun shoved in my face?"

"Yes."

"It's not important."

"Try me."

Benny dropped his head, stared at his bedroom floor. "I saw something I probably shouldn't have. It wasn't right. It turned my stomach."

"What did you see?"

Benny steadied himself, then let out a long, deep breath. "There's a lady who lives in the next building over. Every once and a while I see her with her daughter. The kid's handicapped. I don't know what happened to her, some kind of accident maybe. Anyway, I'm walking home the other night and I see them in front of building B. A few of the Diamondbacks were messing with them. I watched them kick out the kid's canes, not just once, but three times. The third time she fell. She must have hit her head or something because she never got up. Her mother started screaming and calling for help."

"What did you do?"

Benny shook his head, answered in a whisper. "That's the thing. I did absolutely nothing. That's when I knew."

"Knew what?"

"That I didn't want to be part of this life anymore. I'm

not like them. Never have been, never will be. It's not in my nature to want to hurt someone."

"Yet you're a Diamondback."

"Not because I want to be. Because I *have* to be."

"How is it you know so much about Forsythe's operation?"

"He trusts me."

"Why?"

"Who do think my old man went to prison for?"

"Forsythe?"

Benny nodded. "The day he went inside, Forsythe put out the word that he wanted to see me, so I went to his office. He told me he'd made a promise to my dad for doing the time he should have been doing. He gave me a promotion, so to speak. Made me one of his untouchables."

"Untouchables?"

"Same as being a made man in the mafia, only I didn't have to kill anyone to prove my loyalty. My job is to be his eyes and ears on the street. Everyone knows if they fuck with me it's a death sentence for them."

"But you're just a kid. They're grown men."

"Yeah, I know. But that's how it is."

Matt paused. "You said you wanted out."

Benny nodded. "More than anything."

"I can make that happen."

"No, you can't."

"Why not?"

"Like I said before, this is a cradle-to-grave thing. Once a Diamondback, always a Diamondback. The only way anyone ever gets out in a coffin."

Matt stood, walked to Benny's bedroom door, opened it. "I wouldn't be so sure about that."

Benny shook his head. "You're playing with fire," he warned.

"Maybe," Matt replied. "But I'm not the one about to get burned."

Benny watched Matt leave, heard the apartment door close. He hurried down the hallway, fastened the deadbolts.

His grandmother called out. "Benny?"

"Yes, Gran?"

"Would you be a dear and make me a cup of tea?"

Benny followed his grandmother's voice into the living room, saw her sitting in her favorite chair, watching her favorite soap opera. He kissed her on her head. "Sure thing, Gran," he replied.

He suddenly realized he was feeling something he hadn't felt for a very long time.

Hope.

43

Far Too Long

MATT'S PHONE RANG as he left the Building C apartment complex. The number on the display was one he did not recognize. He answered the call, said nothing, waited for the caller to speak.

"Matt, are you there? It's me, Kyla."

"Kyla?"

"Yeah. You okay?"

"Fine."

"Sorry for catching you off guard with this number. I had to toss my phone. I'm using a burner now."

"Why?"

"We have a problem. It's Ferriman."

"What about him?"

"He called. He says he's giving me the day to bring you in

before the Alpha order is opened to the field, but we both know what that really means."

"He's already done it."

"Exactly."

"Have you reached out to your contact to arrange transportation out of the country?"

"That's next on my list. I wanted to let you know about Ferriman first. You need to keep your eyes open, Matt. The situation's changed. I don't know who's been assigned to come after you, but you can bet a damn they'll be one of the best."

"They'll have to be."

"Did you find the kid?"

"Yeah."

"And?"

"He told me what I needed to know."

"What are you going to do?"

"What needs to be done."

"Let it go, Matt," Kyla urged. "You've got more important things to worry about right now than helping some family you hardly know. Namely, staying alive."

"There's more to it than that. There are people here who are in trouble, and it's all because of one man. I can't turn my back on them when I know I can help. I won't."

Kyla sighed. "There's nothing I can say that's going to change your mind, is there?"

"No, there isn't," Matt replied. "This is my fight, Kyla, not yours. You don't have to be part of it. Quite frankly, you shouldn't be. Maybe it's best if you walk away from this assignment... from me. Wait until the morning, then call Ferriman. Tell him you came up empty and recommend he open the order. That will put you in the clear and alleviate

GOOD AS DEAD

any suspicion he may have that you haven't been playing by the rules. I'm not going to drag you down with me. This is my decision. I know what's at stake. I've been responsible for ending many lives during my career with the agency. Whatever I do going forward will be on my terms, not theirs. If they want to come after me, they better bring their A game. If it's a war they want, I'll give them one. Either way, I'm finishing this today."

"I understand," Kyla replied. "I feel the same way. This job has eaten me alive and spat me out. But when your file came up on my phone, I realized maybe it happened for a reason. We've been passing each other in the night for far too long. I don't want to feel that way anymore. I'd rather be with you than without you. So, if it's all the same to you, I'd like to stick around for a while. I can hear the passion in your voice. I can tell that you really want to help these people."

"Yes, I do."

"Then we'll do it together."

Matt thought about the ramifications of what Kyla's decision would mean for her. "Are you absolutely sure about that?"

"I am."

"This is going to get dirty and bloody. Once it starts, there'll be no turning back."

"Is that supposed to frighten me? Please, Matt. In our world, that's just another day at the office."

"I guess it is. All right, you're in."

"What do you need me to do?"

"Are you at my place now?"

"Yes."

"Stay there. Wait for me. I want to visit the family, check

217

in on them, make sure they're okay. You can come with me. I'll introduce you."

"Sounds like a plan."

"Give me thirty minutes."

"I'll be waiting."

44

Badger

FERRIMAN'S DESK PHONE rang. Its display panel identified the caller: **CROSS**. When the task force chief called, the conversation was usually confrontational and rarely ended well. He steadied himself, answered. "Ferrim—"

TFC Cross didn't wait for him to finish speaking. "Why haven't I received an update on Reaper?"

"The situation is fluid, Chief."

"What does that mean? I thought you assigned Reese to find him. You assured me that she would."

"She's been unsuccessful so far, sir."

"Where is she?"

"New York City."

"Why there?"

"It's where she believes Reaper would most likely go to ground."

"Does predictive analysis support that theory?"

"Reaper has operated all over the world, sir. In this case, PA could be unreliable."

"What's your confidence level where Reese is concerned?"

"I trust her judgement, sir."

"Apparently more than I trust yours."

"Sir?"

"You want to know what I've been doing for the last twenty-four hours?"

Ferriman said nothing, waited for Cross to continue as he knew he would.

"Listening to my phone blow up. Everyone in this organization who matters a damn wants to know why the hell we were unsuccessful in eliminating Abdel Gutierrez when we had the chance and how we plan to rectify the situation. Reaper's going rogue only made matters worse. You need to execute a better plan, and you need to do it now."

"I'm working on it, sir."

"Meaning?"

"I've tightened Reese's window. She has until midnight to locate Reaper and escort him to a safe house."

"And if she fails?"

"I don't think she will."

"Well, that's where we have one *mother* of a difference of opinion."

"Sir?"

"Reaper's too good, too smart. Deploying just one asset to find him won't cut it. I'm widening the order. You said Reese believes Reaper is in New York City?"

"Correct."

"Fine. As of this second, she no longer has operational exclusivity. Who's our best stationary asset in New York?"

"That would be Badger, sir."

"Activate him now. Send him Reaper's file."

"Copy that."

"One last thing."

"Sir?"

"Fair warning, Ferriman. Get this done today. If you can't, I'll find someone who can."

"Yes, sir."

Cross hung up.

Ferriman stared at his phone, then placed a call.

PETER HANSON, aka Badger, stared into the massive gaping mouth of the life-sized model of the prehistoric shark on display at the American Museum of Natural History. In his downtime, visiting the museum was his favorite thing to do. Like the megalodon looming before him, the CIA assassin felt at home among the deadly predators featured in this exhibit, primarily because he too was one.

He felt his agency phone vibrate, removed it from its case, thumbed in, opened the file, reviewed the target package information:

SUBJECT: **Gamble, Matt**
    Code Name: REAPER
    Directive: Alpha Level 1
    Priority: C/K

Possible Location: Soundview, New York City

C/K: *Capture/Kill.* Hanson coded out. Before leaving the display, he removed his personal phone from his jacket pocket, positioned himself in front of the prehistoric beast, took a selfie, then left the museum in search of his prey.

45

A Place To Hide

THE WHITE NAVIGATOR stopped outside the gated entrance to the Forest Hills Towers construction site. Darnell Edwards exited the vehicle, unlocked the padlock, removed the security chain, rolled the gate aside, waited for the SUV to drive through, then rejoined Glenn and Evans. Together with Francesca, they drove through the grounds.

Evans soon stopped the car, put it into Park, pointed to the unoccupied site supervisor's trailer. "Let's put her in there for now," he said. "The boss can decide what he wants to do with her when he gets here."

Glenn produced a knife from his jacket pocket, glanced at the teenager seated beside him, warned her. "Try to scream, I'll cut you. Try to run, I'll cut you. Try any shit at all, I'll cut you. Understand?"

Francesca glared at him, said nothing.

"I'll take that as a yes," he said. "Now get out."

The enforcer opened the door, stepped out.

Francesca followed, glanced around, took in her surroundings. She had memorized the meandering route the car had taken through the site, estimated her run time back to the main entrance to be thirty seconds or less at an all-out sprint. All she needed to do was separate herself from her kidnappers by a few feet, just enough room to make a break for it.

Glenn grabbed her arm. "This way."

Francesca made her move. She kicked out as hard and fast as she could. Her foot made solid contact with Glenn's shin. He cried out in pain, dropped the knife, fell to the ground.

Francesca ran for her life.

Glenn's colleagues ran to his aid. "Never mind me," he yelled as they helped him to his feet. He watched Francesca round the corner of the construction trailer as fast as her legs would carry her and disappear out of sight. "Find that fucking bitch!"

Evans and Edwards took chase. The weight of Edwards cast hindered his pursuit.

"There!" Evans called out. "The dump truck!"

Francesca ran past the massive machine, stopped to catch her breath, searched for a place to hide, spied a construction crane several hundred yards in the distance. It was a risky move. She would be in the open, exposed. But she had one advantage Forsythe's men did not have.

She was fast as hell.

Not wasting a second, Francesca made a beeline for the machine, reached it faster than she thought she would, then hid behind its concrete foundation. She looked up, spied the operator's cab at the top of its tower, considered her options. She could climb the tower and hide in the cab, but that would take time and leave her in the open. Besides, she was deathly afraid of heights. One misstep and she would fall to her death. No, there had to be a second option. She saw it on the opposite side of the site, a discarded pile of lumber, its highest board a foot from the top rail of a chain link perimeter fence. If she could scale the timbers, she could jump to the top of the fence, swing herself over the top rail, climb down the other side, and run until she found a police officer. She listened carefully for telltale sounds of her pursuers, heard none. The construction site had fallen eerily quiet. Most disturbing to her was the realization that she was alone with them on the vast parcel of land. There were no work crews assigned to the project yet. For the time being, it remained a ghost site. Nor was there anyone to reach out to for help in this part of town. This was Diamondback territory. Even if she escaped, strangers would avert their eyes, turn their backs on her cries for help. She would need to find someone she could trust to protect her, keep her from harm.

She made her decision when Evans and Edwards came into view and the men drew their weapons.

Francesca looked around. There was no way she could make it to the woodpile without getting shot.

Forty feet away...

She picked up a rock, waited until the men looked away, then tossed it with all her might at the woodpile.

Thirty feet away...

The rock bounced off the timbers. Francesca watched the two men raise their weapons, point them in the direction of the sound. Evans motioned to Edwards, gestured with his hand. The men split up.

Twenty feet away...

Francesca watched them disappear from view. She crawled around the crane's concrete foundation, peered out, searched for them.

Clear.

She needed to take advantage of the distraction she had successfully created and double back the way she had come. There had to be another exit out of the construction site. If there was, she was sure as hell going to find it.

Voices in the distance now, followed by the sound of tumbling wood. The men were investigating the timber pile, overturning it, searching for her.

Now or never.

Francesca ran, then stopped dead in her tracks as a voice called out.

"Don't you fucking move!"

Glenn had found her.

Francesca turned, faced the thug. His weapon was trained on her. He ordered her to the ground. "On your knees."

With no choice but to comply, Francesca dropped to the ground.

The enforcer called out again. Seconds later, he was joined by Evans and Edwards. "Take her inside and tie her up, then leave us alone," he demanded. "Sweet Pea and me got some unfinished business to attend to."

The two men pulled her to her feet, dragged her to the construction trailer, threw her inside, closed the door.

Glenn removed Francesca's medical bracelet from his

pocket, tossed it to Evans. "Take this. Deliver it to the kid's grandparents."

Evans challenged him. "The boss asked you to do that, not me."

"I don't give a rat's ass what he asked me to do," Glenn replied. He glanced at the construction trailer. "I got plans."

"He won't be happy about this," Evans said. "Not one bit."

Glenn walked toward him, raised his weapon, threatened him. "Who's going to tell him? You?"

Evans stared at the man, then shook his head. "No."

Glenn lowered the gun. "That's what I thought. Now get moving."

"Should Edwards come with me?"

"Why? You need a babysitter? That too much for you to handle?"

"Of course not."

"Edwards stays with me," Glenn said sharply. "Someone needs to watch the gate while Sweet Pea and I get better acquainted."

"You better not touch the girl," Evan warned.

"Do us both a favor," Glenn said as he walked up the trailer steps and opened the door. "Mind your fucking business."

46

Classified

MATT KEPT A close eye on the street as he returned to his townhouse from Building C and his meeting with Benny Ortiz. New York City was enjoying a typical day. The roads were busy with traffic, the street level shops filled with customers. Where groups of people walked in close proximity to one another, Matt slipped in behind them, kept his head down, tried to blend in. Crowds offered cover, and right now cover was his only ally. His conversation with Benny Ortiz kept repeating in his mind. The kid didn't deserve the lousy hand life had dealt him. If he could, he would make good on his promise to help him find a way to a better life. But first, he had to stay alive long enough to do so.

He crossed the street several houses down from his own property, scoped it out for signs it had been compromised, saw none. The thought that it might have been sent a chill down his spine. Kyla was inside. If his townhouse had been identified and infiltrated, she might already be dead. In the agency's pursuit of Alpha Level 1 targets, collateral damage was factored in. Locating the target and completing the mission was everything. The assigned asset, or team, would enter the property, clear the house at speed, and find and eliminate the target. The operation would be executed with military precision, the killing clinical, without conscience. Despite being a highly trained operative herself, it was possible Kyla might not even get off a single round before her life ended. From the street level walk up to the front door, his home appeared secure, although it was still possible that the rear entrance had been compromised. For the moment that would not be a concern. He had visually cleared the front of the property. He took out his phone, called Kyla's burner.

"Hello?"

Matt spoke the safe words he and Kyla had agreed upon years ago in the event of an emergency. If one suspected the other had been compromised, the wrong response would be given, and the mission terminated. He hoped she would remember her code and reply accordingly. "Parachute. October. Pencil. Garden," he said.

Kyla paused, remembered the required response. "Skydive. July. Typewriter. Forest. You're good, Matt. All clear."

Matt walked up the stairs. Kyla opened the door, met him in the front entrance. "Any problems besides the kid?" she asked.

"Someone's going to need a stitch or two."

"As long as that someone isn't you, I don't care."

"You up for a field trip?" Matt asked.

"Where to?"

"I want to check in on the Vitagliano's, see how they're doing."

"The family from the fire?"

"Yeah."

"You know where they live?"

Matt nodded. "I hailed a cab for them the night of the fire. I memorized the address Domenic gave the driver. It's only a few blocks from here, but I'd prefer to drive, not walk."

"I agree. You need to stay out of sight until we leave tonight."

"Were you able to reach your contact?"

"I did. His name is Oleg Schroeder."

"What's the plan?"

"You know the Tiffany Street Pier on the East River?"

"Yeah. Off Barretto Point Park."

"We're to be there at midnight. A fishing charter will pick us up. The name of his boat is *Off The Hook*. Schroeder will provide us with our documents and new IDs."

"And then?"

"The charter will take us out a few miles offshore. From there, we'll transfer to a go-fast boat. It will take us to our intercept point."

"Which is?"

"A container ship returning to Honduras called *Goliath*. The go-fast will pull up alongside her while she's at speed. We'll board via rope ladder."

"How do we get from the Goliath into Honduras?"

"Schroeder's arranged with Goliath's captain to have a second go-fast boat meet the ship before it enters Honduran waters. It will take us to shore. We're on our own from there."

Matt smiled. "Couldn't have just booked a flight, huh?"

Kyla laughed. "Hardly."

"You ready?"

Kyla slipped into her jacket. "Ready."

"Wait for me," Matt said. He opened the front door, checked the street. It was quiet. He walked down the stairs, placed his thumb on the garage door's biometric identification lock. The vault-style pins integrated into the armor-plated steel door retracted from the cement floor. The door rose. Matt slipped into the garage, started the van, pulled out. Kyla locked the townhouse door, seated herself in the van. Matt waited for the garage door to descend and lock into place. Together they left for the Vitagliano's.

DOMENIC AND CARLA'S home was much more upscale than Matt's. The single-family townhouse featured a ten step walk up from the street to a landing surrounded by an ornate iron railing. The double-wide mahogany entrance doors added to its character and curb appeal. However, the wrought iron security grates which protected its windows served as a reminder that the neighborhood was no longer as safe as it once had been.

Matt parked his old van on the street in front of the Vitagliano's property, walked with Kyla up the steps to the front door, rang the doorbell.

Domenic answered the door. He was surprised to see his new friend standing on his doorstep.

"Matt," he said. "What are you doing here? How did you know where I live?"

"I remembered the address you gave the cab driver the other night."

"Right. The cab. I forgot."

"I'm sorry, Domenic," Matt said. "I hope I'm not disturbing you. I just wanted to check on you and your family, make sure you're all right."

Carla joined her husband at the door. She wore a tired expression on her face. Matt could see she had been crying.

Something was wrong.

"Carla?" Matt asked. "Are you all right?"

Carla covered her mouth with her hand, shook her head, said nothing, turned away.

A terrible feeling swept over Matt. He challenged his friend. "What's going on, Domenic?" he asked. "Where's Francesca?"

"I'm sorry, Matt," Domenic replied. "It's not a good time for us. You'll have to come back later." He tried to close the door.

Matt stopped it with his hand. "I'm not going anywhere until you tell me what's wrong," he said.

Domenic tried to maintain a brave face, but the stress and anxiety of the situation got the better of him. He retrieved Francesca's braided cord medical bracelet from his pocket, handed it to Matt. "It's Francesca's," he said. "One of Forsythe's men delivered it here a few minutes ago. He told me if I don't do what Forsythe told me to do, we'll never see her again."

Matt stepped through the door, noticed the study located just inside the front door. He took his friend by the arm, guided him to his chair. Kyla followed. "Easy,

Domenic," Matt said. "Tell me exactly what's going on. Don't leave anything out."

Domenic gathered himself, fought back his tears, drew a deep breath, exhaled slowly. "Forsythe wants me to go to the police and tell them it was me who started the fire. If I don't, he'll kill Francesca."

"He said that?"

Domenic nodded. "The hall closet. My windbreaker. Check the pocket."

Matt walked to the closet, found the jacket, rifled through the pockets, pulled out a crumpled photograph of Francesca, stared at it. "I don't understand," he said.

"Forsythe's men picked me up and took me to a construction site. That picture was taped to a wall which he destroyed with a wrecking ball. He told me he'd replace the picture with Francesca and kill her." Domenic's voice trembled. "Francesca never takes that bracelet off, Matt. She knows she can't. He has her. That bastard has my granddaughter."

Matt put the picture in his pocket. "This construction site. Do you know where it is?"

Domenic nodded. "I saw a sign outside the main gate. Forest Hill Towers. It's four blocks west of the mission." He tried to stand. "Please, Matt. I have to go."

"You're not going anywhere, Domenic," Matt replied. "I'll take care of this."

Domenic shook his head. "You can't. Forsythe and his men will kill you."

"I wouldn't be so sure about that," Matt replied. He turned to Kyla. "Stay with them. Keep them safe. I'll be back as soon as I've found the girl."

"Copy that," Kyla replied.

"*Copy that?*" Domenic said. "Who talks like that? Who are you really, Matt? And who is this woman?"

Kyla answered. "My name is Kyla, Mr. Vitagliano. I'm an associate of Matt's."

"What kind of associate?"

"All I can tell you is that we work for the government."

"In what capacity?"

Matt answered. "I'm afraid that's classified, Domenic."

"I knew from the moment we met there was something different about you," Domenic said. "I just couldn't put my finger on it."

"Now you know," Matt said. "But I need you to do me a favor."

"Of course."

"You can't tell anyone."

Domenic nodded. "Your secret is safe with us."

"Good. Now forget about going to the police. You're not going to admit to something you didn't do."

"But Francesca..."

Matt put his hand on his friend's shoulder. "Don't worry about Francesca. I'll find her." Matt stood. He turned to Kyla as he left the room. "I'll be back as soon as I can. In the meantime, no one other than me comes through that door. Got it?"

Kyla nodded. "Got it."

47

Two Possible Explanations

SEATED BEHIND THE wheel of his black Dodge Charger on the street outside the American Museum of Natural History, Badger heard his cell phone's notification bell sound. He had received a message. He thumbed in, read the message, viewed the attachment. Ferriman had a reason for dispatching him so quickly. According to the communique, the possibility existed that the operative assigned to bring in Reaper may have been compromised. Kyla Reese's picture stared back at him from the screen. She was a highly respected assassin whom he had known only by her code name, Sparrow. Now there were two targets. Although the directive issued against Reese did not include a capture/kill order, Ferriman wanted her detained. She was to return to Langley for immediate debriefing with Ferriman and Task

Force Chief Cross. He was to locate her, learn all he could from her about where she suspected Reaper might have gone underground, then proceed with eliminating the target if he failed to comply with the agency's order to come in. Reese's field record showed she had taken a hotel room in Soundview. A clickable link in the encrypted message provided him with a map of New York City and her cell phone's present location. He watched as the blue dot on the screen traveled north. She was currently on White Plains Road, headed towards Little Yemen. He punched the destination into the car's GPS. She was forty-five minutes away. Badger pulled out of his parking spot, entered the traffic flow.

As he navigated the vehicular waters of the city, he imagined himself as the prehistoric shark he had just admired in the museum exhibit. Like him, it too had been aware of its position atop the food chain, restless, constantly on the move, living for the next kill. Only a handful of men and women on the planet were as uniquely qualified to do this job as he was, and fewer still were as good at it. In his tenure as a field operative, he had amassed an impressive one-hundred-and-seventy kills, all of which had been completed domestically against enemies of the state operating on American soil. This was the first assignment he had received that would have him tracking down two of his own. No matter. A kill was a kill. He knew better than to overthink the situation. The practice had become routine for him now. Locate the target, move in, execute, exfiltrate. He had become such an expert in blending into his surroundings that he had garnered a second nickname at the agency: The Ghost. He preferred Badger. The characteristics and temperament of the animal better suited him: stocky, powerfully built, ferocious, nocturnal, clever, tenacious, undaunted in its pursuit of its prey.

The GPS began to beep. Badger suddenly realized that he had become so absorbed in his own thoughts he had lost track of time. Forty minutes had passed. The blue dot on the screen showed Reese was not far from him now, just a few car lengths ahead.

Badger accelerated, studied the occupants in the vehicles as he passed them. All males, no females.

He changed lanes quickly, pulled in behind a garbage truck.

The blue light which indicated Reese's cellular position flashed rapidly, then turned solid blue. There were only two possible explanations for this. Either Reese's phone was with her body in the back of the garbage truck, or she had ditched the device with the intention of throwing prospective pursuers off her trail.

Badger waited for a break in the traffic, then raced ahead of the garbage truck, cut it off, jumped out of his car.

The driver locked up the vehicle's brakes. The truck shuddered to a stop. He threw open his door, jumped down from his cab, yelled at Badger. "Are you crazy, man? I could have run you over!"

Badger ignored the man, walked past him, inspected the back of the truck, saw no signs of blood in the rig's packer or tailgate. If Reese's body had been dumped in the back of the truck and compacted, grisly evidence of it would have been visible.

"Sorry," Badger said as he walked past the driver and returned to his car. "My bad."

Either Reese had tossed her phone or Reaper had.

Badger jumped behind the wheel, dropped the car into

gear, pulled a quick U-turn, headed south. There was only one thing he could do now. He would go to Reese's hotel room. If she was there, he would make her take him to Reaper. If she wasn't, he would toss her room, search for clues to the target's whereabouts, then find him.

He punched the gas, resumed the hunt.

48

Cover

AS MATT REACHED the future home of Forest Hill Towers, he slowed the van. The condominium construction project, which had not yet started, encompassed a city block. The marketing billboards which surrounded the property served to keep curiosity seekers at bay while their glossy architectural images depicted the prestigious lifestyle the future property promised.

The main construction entrance was situated off the main road. Matt circled the block in search of an alternate access point to the site. He found it in an alley on the north side of the property. Vandals had punched a hole through a section of a plywood barricade in order to gain access to the property, then covered it up with a loose board. Matt assumed their intention was to scour the site in search of copper wiring, pipe, or construction tools; anything of value that could be sold or pawned. He put the van in Park, jumped out, moved the board aside, inspected the opening.

He could fit through it, no problem.

Matt backed the van up against the barricade, covered the hole with the vehicle's sliding side door, then slipped out of the driver's seat and into the cargo compartment. He unlocked the metal chest behind the driver's seat, removed the ordnance and tactical gear he would need, slipped a bulletproof vest over his head, adjusted its velcro straps to fit him snuggly, filled the vest pockets with an assortment of knives and spare clips, fitted a sound suppressor to the barrel of his Sig Sauer handgun, chambered a round. He had no idea what he would be up against once he breached the site and headed off in search of Francesca. He wasn't taking any chances. The Diamondbacks had a reputation for violence, and if that was what they wanted, he would be only too happy to accommodate them.

Now completely hidden from sight, Matt slid open the van's side door, moved aside the wooden board, slipped through the hole into the construction site, then listened for sounds of activity or voices which would give away their position. He heard it seconds later. A disturbance. Two men arguing. The commotion was interrupted by a faint scream. Matt recognized the voice. It was Francesca.

Matt raised his weapon, stayed low and front sight focused, and quickly navigated the unfamiliar terrain of the construction site, clearing each blind corner until he reached the location of the sound. He dropped to one knee behind the concrete bed of a crane, peered around the corner, sighted the men. One stood on the bottom step of a construction trailer, pointing his finger up at the other, yelling. A second man looked down, yelled back. Inside the trailer, he heard Francesca. She was crying.

Maintaining cover, Matt ran toward the rear of the trailer, reached it, sighted a window, peered inside. Francesca sat on a chair directly ahead, her back to him. Her kidnapper stood in the open doorway, deeply entrenched in the heated verbal exchange.

Matt tapped lightly on the window, tried to get Francesca's attention. On his third attempt, she turned, saw him, started to rise out of her chair. He raised his hand, motioned for her to sit, then brought a finger to his lips. Francesca understood, nodded, sat. Matt raised the Sig. Slowly, he rounded the corner of the building and confronted the men.

Edwards stood at the foot of the construction trailer stairs, arguing with Glenn. Matt's sudden appearance took him by surprise. He stared at the assassin and the weapon being leveled at him, fell silent.

"What?" Glenn yelled. "You got nothin' else to say? What happened to all the tough talk?"

Edwards swallowed hard.

"What's your fucking problem?" Glenn yelled.

Edwards said nothing.

"Hey, asshole! Answer me!"

"Your girlfriend can't talk right now," Matt announced. "He's too busy pissing himself."

Glenn's head shot out from behind the open door. He glanced at Matt. "You!" he yelled. He tried to duck inside, but Matt was too fast.

Matt turned his weapon toward the base of the door, fired a silent round.

Glenn screamed. He fell forward out of the construction

trailer and tumbled down the stairs, his left tibia and fibula jointly shattered by the bullet. He hit the ground, rolled onto his back, tried to scamper away. His hand moved to his waist to retrieve his weapon. Matt fired again. The second round tore through his forearm. Glenn's arm fell limply to his side.

Matt advanced on the fallen man. "So, you like to play with young girls, huh?" he said.

Glenn's tough guy persona had evaporated. "I was never going to hurt her," he pleaded. "Just mess with her a little."

"Mess with her?" Matt said. "Is that your definition of rape?"

Glenn shook his head. "I swear I was never going to do anything like that!"

"You know what?" Matt asked.

"What?" Glenn cried.

Matt lowered the weapon, pressed the sound suppressor against Glenn's forehead. "I don't believe you." He fired. The man's body jumped. He was dead.

Matt turned, faced Francesca's second kidnapper. "Who else is here?" he asked.

Edwards shook his head. "Nobody!"

Matt raised the gun, pointed it at him.

"I swear to God!" Edwards yelled. "It's just me, Glenn, and the girl!"

"Where's Forsythe?"

"I don't know!"

"Bullshit."

"I'm telling the truth!"

"Is he at Red Thunder?"

Edwards looked shocked. "How did you know about—"

"Good talk," Matt said. He pulled the trigger, put a

round in the man's head, watched him drop to the ground, then called out. "Francesca?"

No reply.

Matt raised his gun, walked cautiously up the stairs, cleared the construction trailer entrance door left and right, found the Vitagliano's granddaughter curled up under a desk.

Matt leaned over, spoke to the teen. "It's okay," he said. "It's over now. You're safe. Those men can't hurt you anymore." He extended his hand. "What do you say we get you back home to your grandparents?"

Francesca nodded, grabbed her backpack, crawled out from under the desk, stood.

Matt warned her. "When we go outside, keep your eyes closed until I tell you to open them. Will you do that for me?"

Francesca wiped away her tears. Her response came as a whisper. "Okay."

Matt held the teenager for a moment, comforted her. "All right," he said. "Let's go."

49

Mr. Random Guy

MATT COVERED FRANCESCA'S eyes as he led her down the stairs and past the two dead men. Together, they hurried through the construction site to the hole in the billboard. He followed the teen through the van's open side door, returned the loose board to its position, closed the door.

Francesca moved into the passenger seat as Matt slipped out of the bulletproof vest, opened the armaments lock box, and returned his gear to their respective compartments. He took his place in the driver's seat, turned to the girl. Francesca was shaking. In the commotion, she had left her jacket in the trailer.

Matt slipped out of his BulletBlocker jacket, wrapped the coat around her. "There," he said. "It's not exactly a blanket, but it will keep you warm. You'll be home soon." Her torn blouse prompted him to ask an uncomfortable question. "Francesca, did he...?"

Francesca shook her head. "He tried, but he never got the chance. The other guy, his partner, or whatever he was, kept him away from me."

Matt nodded. "Good."

"I wanted to kill him so badly," the teen said. "I would have if I'd had the opportunity. But he was so much bigger and stronger than me." She ran her hand down her bruised arm. "I tried to get to the pepper spray Grandpa had bought for me. It was in my jacket pocket. As soon as I pulled it out he knocked it out of my hand. It slid under the desk. I guess that's when he realized I wasn't going to let him do to me what he wanted to without putting up a fight. That's when he started to choke me. The other guy must have heard me because he came into the trailer and pulled him off me. He tried to fight him, but with a broken arm he couldn't. It was enough to make him back off, though. After that, they argued the whole time until you showed up." Francesca paused. "How did you know where I was?"

Matt realized this was not the time to share Domenic's previous ordeal with her. "You can thank your grandfather for that. I'll let him explain everything to you later. Right now, we need to get out of here." He started the van, pulled away from the billboard.

Francesca glanced at him as they drove. "You're a policeman, aren't you?" she asked.

Matt checked his mirrors, made sure they hadn't been followed since leaving Forest Hill Towers construction site. "What makes you say that?"

"Seriously? I might only be sixteen, but I recognize a bulletproof vest when I see one."

Matt grinned. "Picked it up at a yard sale. Never thought it would come in handy. Guess I was wrong."

"Yard sale, my ass."

"Army surplus?"

"Try again."

"No, Francesca. I'm not a policeman."

Francesca pressed. "Military? Navy SEAL?"

"No, not a cop, not military, not a SEAL."

"I've got it. You're a superhero." She glanced in the back of the van. "I'll bet you've got a cape and cowl stashed back there, right?"

Matt shook his head, smiled. "No such luck."

"So, you're just some random guy who goes around disarming people in homeless missions and rescuing abducted teenagers?"

"The randomest."

Francesca sighed. "You're really not going to tell me who you are, are you?"

"I thought we just established who I am."

"Mr. Random Guy."

"Exactly."

Francesca sat quietly, stared out the window as they drove, then spoke. "You know what you could really use?"

"What's that?"

"A new ride."

"You don't like the van?"

"It's a million years old."

"Not quite."

"And a cape. You definitely need a cape."

"I don't really go in for that sort of thing."

"Every superhero needs a cape."

"I'm not a—"

"Yeah, you are. To me at least."

Matt smiled. "I'll take the compliment."

"So you should."

Matt turned at the lights, headed down Francesca's street toward her home.

"Is there a Mrs. Random Guy?" she asked.

Matt shook his head. "You ask a lot of questions, you know that?"

Francesca smiled. "I'm sixteen. I'm supposed to. Well, is there?"

"No."

"A *soon-to-be* Mrs. Random Guy?"

"You don't let up, do you?"

"It's part of my charm."

"Is that so?"

"Yep. So, what's holding you back?"

"It's complicated."

"Binary operations, vector calculus, and matrix algebra is complicated. Love isn't."

"I have no idea what you just said."

"It's math."

"I'll take your word for it."

"The future Mrs. Random Guy isn't going to wait forever, you know."

"I know."

"Then get a move on, already!"

Matt pulled up in front of the Vitagliano's town-home. "We're here," he said. "And not a moment too soon."

Francesca smiled. "Too much straight talk for one ride, huh?"

Matt turned to the teen, unbuckled his seatbelt, tossed it

aside. "I feel sorry for your boyfriend. He's in way over his head."

"Boyfriend?" Francesca asked, then winked. "What boyfriend?"

Matt smiled. "Got it."

Francesca opened her door.

"Hold up," Matt said. "Stay in the van. I want to clear the street first."

"You think we were followed?"

"No, but I'm not taking any chances."

"Okay."

Matt exited the vehicle. Nothing around him seemed out of place. He took out his phone, called Kyla. "Confirmation?"

"Skydive. July. Typewriter. Forest," Kyla answered.

"Copy that."

Matt glanced at Francesca, gave her a thumbs up.

The teen exited the van, ran up the front steps of her grandparent's townhouse, fell into their waiting arms. Domenic and Carla held her tight.

"Are you okay, sweetheart?" Domenic asked.

Francesca looked up, smiled. "I'm fine, Grandpa," she said. "Thanks to Matt."

Matt walked up the steps behind her, entered the home.

Domenic looked at Matt, held back his tears. "I don't know what to say. Thank you for bringing her home."

Matt smiled. "Don't mention it."

Francesca looked past her grandparents, saw Kyla, smiled. "You must be the future Mrs. Random Guy," she said.

Kyla looked at Matt quizzically.

Matt laughed. "Don't ask. You ready?"

Kyla nodded. "Yes."

Matt turned to the family. "We'll be back. In the meantime, keep the doors locked and stay away from the windows."

Francesca removed Matt's jacket, handed it back to him. "Where are you going?" she asked.

Matt opened the door. Kyla followed.

"To find Forsythe," he replied.

50

Paloma Helo Bravo

BADGER SAT AT the lights, waited for the signal to turn from red to green. Reese's hotel was ten minutes from his present location. If she was there, his job would be a lot less complicated. He would find out what she knew about Reaper and where to find him, or report back to Ferriman that her cooperation had been all but useless and let him decide whether she was still considered of value where the Alpha One Priority was concerned. Ferriman had given him every indication he had his doubts about her. Perhaps she was more involved in the operation than she was letting on. She was a highly trained operative who had come to New York City directly after being assigned the Reaper file. There had to be a reason for that. She had to be doing more than following a hunch. She must have had inside knowledge of Reaper's whereabouts, and that made her dangerous. If she was deliberately keeping Reaper off the radar, she had signed her own death warrant. The directive from Ferriman would be clear: kill them both.

He was drumming the steering wheel to a tune in his head when across the road he watched an old van slow, then turn right. For some reason it caught his attention. He stared at the driver. Something about the van didn't feel right. Like the prehistoric shark in the museum, he too had trained his senses to become constantly aware of his habitat. The man's profile hung on his retina as the van turned the corner, headed down the street. Badger removed his phone and took a second look at the file photo of Reaper attached to the capture/kill order.

No, he thought. It couldn't be this easy.

He proceeded through the light, pulled up to the curb, parked the car, and waited. He watched the van proceed down the street, then come to a stop ten houses down the road. The driver got out, scanned the road, then made a phone call. Seconds later, a young girl exited the vehicle, ran up the stairs, and entered the townhouse. The man looked around, observed his surroundings, followed the girl into the house, and closed the door.

The resemblance to the target was uncanny, but from this distance Badger could not be sure if it was the quarry he sought. He watched the house, removed his mini binoculars from his glove box, read the plate, placed a call.

"Code in, please."

"Paloma Helo Bravo 339."

"Stand by for voice print verification," the operator said.

Badger waited.

"Confirmed. Proceed."

"California commercial license plate. 57941-CM. Requesting registration information."

"Stand by."

The CIA operator returned to the line seconds later: "Vehicle is registered to Perfect Window Cleaning, Loma Vista, California."

"Copy. End." Badger ended the call.

He set down the binoculars, drummed the steering wheel anxiously, talked to himself. "Not enough windows to clean in Loma Vista that you had to come all the way to New York City, huh? Bullshit."

The front door opened. A man exited the property, accompanied by a woman. He recognized Kyla Reese immediately.

"Well, I'll be damned," he said. "Gotcha."

Badger waited until the van pulled away from the curb, then followed.

51

Out Of Nowhere

FOLLOWING THE TIP that Benny Ortiz had provided, Matt and Kyla drove to Hunt's Point. Matt cruised the waterfront until he found the building he was looking for.

"There it is," he said. "Red Thunder Fireworks Manufacturing and Special Effects."

"What's so special about this place?" Kyla asked.

"It's not what it appears to be."

"It appears to be a manufacturer of things that go boom. I assume I'm missing something?"

"You are."

"Care to fill me in?"

"The company you see is legit. It's what you can't see that isn't."

"Which is?"

"What's below it. There's a basement hidden from view which comprises the biggest meth lab in all of New York City. It's run by the same waste of skin who orchestrated the firebombing of the Vitagliano's mission and ordered Francesca's kidnapping, David Forsythe. It's where he manufactures Sapphire Slam, his designer form of crystal meth. It's also his main source of income and what fuels his business and real estate empire."

"How do you know this?"

"The kid I met with yesterday, Benny Ortiz. He told me."

"Are you sure he wasn't lying to you?"

Matt nodded. "He spent enough time staring down the barrel of my Sig to know better than to do that. Besides, I can always tell when someone is lying to me. He wasn't."

"But isn't he one of Forsythe's gang?"

"He is, but he wants out. I'm going to help him do that."

Matt spied movement outside the building. A figure walked to the corner of the facility, looked around, turned back. "Looks like Forsythe has a sentry patrolling the grounds," he said. "Maybe more than one."

"Are you sure it's not just an employee of the fireworks company?" Kyla asked. "You did say it's a legitimate operation."

"I did. But look at the sign on the lawn."

Kyla read the company's business hours and days of operation. "They're only open four days a week."

Matt nodded. "And today's not one of them. Care to guess what they're doing in there now?"

"Making meth."

"Precisely." Matt pointed down the road. "Check it out."

Matt and Kyla watched as a pearl blue Bentley Continental GT entered the parking lot. The driver stepped out, alarmed the vehicle, then entered the building through the front door. The Bentley's vanity plate read **DMD DAVE**.

"Our guest of honor has arrived, just like Benny said he would," Matt said.

"He knew Forsythe was coming here?"

Matt nodded. "There's a major shipment of Slam going out today. Forsythe wants to oversee it personally."

"That's bold."

"Too bad it's not gonna happen."

"How do you want to approach this?" Kyla asked.

"I was thinking of walking in through the front door."

"The direct approach. I like it."

"They would never expect it."

"Exactly."

Matt left his seat, moved into the cargo area of the van, unlocked the armaments locker behind his seat. "Time to tac up," he told Kyla.

Kyla joined him in the back of the van. Matt handed her a bulletproof vest, MK13 sniper rifle, sound suppressor, a Sig Sauer P320 pistol and suppressor, spare clips, and an assortment of tactical knives. Kyla fitted the vest to her body, filled its pockets and sleeves with the clips and knives, affixed the suppressors to the weapons. "You came to play," she said.

"You know the old saying," Matt said as he geared up. "Pray for peace..."

"... Prepare for war," Kyla finished.

Outside the van, dusk had infiltrated the evening sky, bruising it in hues of purple and slashes of red.

Matt turned to Kyla. "We do this fast. We get in, deal with Forsythe, then get out."

"What about the lab?"

"Leave that to me."

"Copy that."

"Ready?"

"Ready."

Matt opened the side door of the van, prepared to step out.

The volley of rounds came out of nowhere, struck the passenger window and van door, forced Matt back inside.

"Sonofabitch!" Matt yelled as he slammed the door closed. "Where the hell did that come from?"

Kyla moved into the passenger seat, saw that the van's windows had not been shattered or its body pierced in the assault. "Armored glass?" she asked.

"Is there any other kind?"

"Good thinking. What about the rest of this relic?"

"The panels are ballistic steel plate. So is the roof."

"Tires?"

"Run-flats. Self-sealing."

"Someone's a little paranoid."

"There are a few people out there who'd like to see me dead."

"One of them is doing their damnedest to make that happen right now."

"Ferriman. The Alpha priority."

Kyla nodded. "Someone followed us here."

"Bad for them," Matt said. "I really don't feel like dying today. You?"

"I hadn't planned on it." Kyla glanced at the passenger side mirror, caught a glimpse of the shooter. "Got him," she said. "Five o'clock. Three buildings down. Rooftop. Air conditioning unit."

"You think you have a shot?"

Kyla shook her head. "From in here? Not a chance."

"Then we need to move. Lay down suppressive fire until I get to the building. When I reach the door, I'll do the same, make entry, and find Forsythe. You find that asshole and take him out."

"Copy that."

"On me in three... two... *one.*"

Matt threw open the door and shoulder rolled out of the van as Kyla targeted the shooter and opened fire on the distant rooftop. The sound suppressed rounds from her assault rifle ripped through the air as Matt ran to the front entrance of Red Thunder.

Thwup, thwup, thwup, thwup, thwup, thwup, thwup, thwup, thwup.

Now clear of the assassin's direct line of fire, Matt signaled for Kyla to move. He opened up with his weapon on the building, his rounds plinking off the commercial rooftop air-conditioning unit. The lack of returned fire meant they had either successfully taken out the shooter, pinned him down, or that he was already on the move in search of a better vantage point from which to sight and execute his targets.

As Kyla reached the side of the building, Matt entered Red Thunder.

BADGER FELL in behind the air conditioning unit, heard the whistle of the rounds as they struck the machine. Sparks flew inside the device, and the compressor suddenly stopped humming. Thankfully, Reese had only managed to kill the machine and not him. That was the good news. The bad news was that he had lost sight of them both. Smooth move, bulletproofing the old van, he thought. He hadn't seen that one coming. Reaper just might prove to be harder to kill than expected.

He had followed the van from the teenager's house to the commercial district, watched them park down the street, then scoped out the businesses closest to him. The three-story building where he had parked was the tallest on the street. The complex was empty. He could see no cars in any of the neighboring lots. The employees had left for the day.

He'd lost sight of Reese when he was forced to take cover from Reaper's rounds, and separate targets would only complicate what was quickly escalating into an untenable situation. He needed to reposition himself as soon as possible, reestablish a tactical advantage. Reese was now a clear and present danger. She would have to be eliminated first. It had been his experience that women operatives, although extremely attractive, were always easier to kill than their male counterparts. Despite being equally trained, when it came down to the wire, they hesitated a split-second longer than necessary. He knew this because he had killed many female foreign operatives before they had had the chance to kill him, but certainly not before showing them a very good time.

Badger walked across the building's rooftop to its steel access ladder, trained his weapon down, peered over the edge. Wooden shipping pallets stacked against the neighboring warehouse wall offered the only available cover. He opened fire on them as a precaution, spraying them from top to bottom, left to right, obliterating them all.

No Reese.

Perhaps she had made it back to the van.

He returned to his previous position behind the air conditioner, checked out Reaper's vehicle. The side door still lay open. A trained operative would never do that unless it was a trap.

Patience was his greatest weapon now. He would do what they would least expect him to do, which was to remain exactly where he was. As far as he knew right now, the van was their only means of escape. They would have to return to it sooner or later. When they did, he would eliminate them. Two shots under the cover of night. Like shooting fish in a barrel. Easy peasy. Wham bam, thank you ma'am.

Another pleasant thought occurred to him. Like the megalodon in the museum, eliminating the fabled Matt Gamble would put him at the top of the CIA's covert asset food chain. He was tired of being known as the agency's number two assassin. Tonight's kill suddenly meant more to him than just completing the mission that was his assignment. Tonight, he would make history.

Badger's shoulder cramped. He lowered his rifle, shrugged his shoulder to alleviate the discomfort, rolled his head from side to side, cracked his neck, shook it off, then was shocked to feel a white-hot pain penetrate his neck.

Kyla drove the Ka-Bar knife blade into him as deep as she could, twisted it sharply, held it in place, then removed a second tactical knife from her vest. Badger felt its tip pierce his skin. He gasped as it broke through. Kyla transected his lower back with surgical precision, severed his spinal cord.

Badger's legs gave out.

Kyla eased his now paralyzed body down to the ground,

leaned over, whispered in his ear. "Guess you missed the class on situational awareness, asshole," she said. "There are two access points to this roof, not one."

Badger stared up at the assassin, a look of wide-eyed surprise on his face.

Kyla pulled out the knives, wiped them clean on Badger's leg, returned them to her vest.

Badger forced a smile. "Well, that was unexpected," he said. His breathing grew weak, labored. "Nicely played, Sparrow."

"Who's with you?" Kyla asked as she rifled through the assassin's pockets.

"Nobody."

She retrieved his cell phone, shoved it into her pocket. "That the truth?"

"I'm dying," Badger replied. "What reason would I have to lie?"

"Good point."

"Finish it, Reese."

"I'm going to need something first."

"I figured you might."

Kyla removed the Ka-Bar knife from her vest, covered his mouth to muffle his screams, then cut off his thumbs and shoved them into her pocket. She removed her pistol, attached its silencer, stood, stared down at the man. "You ready?"

"Not really."

Thwup.

Kyla's first round blew out the back of Badger's head.

Thwup, thwup.

The follow up rounds stopped his heart.

Kyla retrieved his assault weapon, hurried to the ladder

she had used to access the rooftop, descended quickly, ran to the van, tossed the killer's rifle inside, raced to Red Thunder's front door, drew her Sig, threw open the door, made entry, cleared the lobby, stopped, and listened.

Matt was nowhere to be seen.

52

An Outstanding Performance

MATT HEARD VOICES on the approach, took cover behind a steel filing cabinet in the hallway, waited until they were just feet away, then stepped into the corridor, raised his weapon, fired twice.

Thwup, thwup.

The silenced headshots dropped the armed sentries before they had the chance to retrieve their weapons. Matt stayed in motion as he delivered the deadly rounds, retrieved an electronic key card from one of the corpses, hurried down the corridor, reached the intersection, cleared it left and right, then paused. He read the sign affixed to a steel door at the far end of the hallway: **DANGER. COMBUSTIBLE MATERIALS. AUTHORIZED PERSONNEL ONLY BEYOND THIS POINT.**

Matt approached the door, tested its handle.

Locked.

Behind him, a sound emanated from the corridor in which he had just dispatched the two guards. He swung around, pressed his body against the wall, pointed his weapon in the direction of the sound, waited.

Kyla peered around the corner.

Matt raised his Sig to the ceiling, signaled to her. Kyla hurried down the hallway, met him at the door.

"You okay?" she whispered.

Matt nodded. "You find the shooter?"

"Yeah."

"Anyone I'd know?"

"Badger."

"You send him on his way?"

Kyla knew what Matt was referring to. "Three times," she said.

"Better safe than sorry."

Kyla nodded. "Is that the lab?"

Matt shook his head. "Benny said there's a sub-basement." He peered through the door's wire reinforced glass window into the massive warehouse. Boxes of fireworks and drums of chemicals were stacked row after row on commercial shelves. "There are enough explosives in there to level a city block," he said.

"Any sign of Forsythe?"

"No. My guess he's in the lab."

"Which is located somewhere *under* the warehouse."

"Exactly."

"I don't suppose Benny told you where to find the entrance?"

"No."

"Wonderful."

"It shouldn't be hard to find."

"I'd prefer a sign on the wall. Something like, *This Way To Meth Lab. Visitors Please Sign In.*"

"That would have been easier," Matt replied. He touched the electronic key card to the door's access pad, pushed down on the door handle, eased it open. "Stay on my six. Ready?"

"Ready."

"Moving."

Matt and Kyla entered the warehouse, moved quickly, cleared the racks, reached the end of the warehouse.

Kyla lowered her assault rifle. "Nothing," she said. "You sure your intel was solid? The kid could have been bullshitting you. Maybe there's no lab here after all."

"He wasn't, and there is."

"You don't know that for certain."

"Yes, I do."

"How?"

"Forsythe."

"What about him?"

"He's not here. Was his car still in the lot when you made entry?"

"Yeah."

"Then he's here somewhere. We just need to draw him out."

"How do you propose we do that?"

"What's the last thing you'd want to have happen in a place like this?"

"A fire."

"Exactly." Matt looked around the warehouse, spotted a tall glass cabinet, walked to it. Inside, rows of full-face gas masks hung on hooks. He opened the door, removed two masks, handed one to Kyla.

Kyla took the mask, stared at Matt. "If you're planning on starting a fire in a fireworks factory I'd kind of like to leave now."

Matt shook his head. "I just want to make it look like there's a fire."

"To flush out Forsythe."

Matt nodded. He searched the warehouse shelves, found the box he was looking for, opened it, removed four canisters labelled M3 RED SMOKE GRENADE, handed two to Kyla. "I'll take the north and east walls; you take the south and west. Pop smoke and come back here."

"And then?"

"We wait."

"Copy." Kyla ran off, deployed the canisters, rejoined Matt.

"Masks," Matt said.

The response was fast. As the thick caustic smoke filled the warehouse, Matt and Kyla were surprised when the very cabinet from which they had retrieved the gas masks suddenly opened outward.

Matt's suppressed rounds felled the first two men as they exited the lab's hidden entrance, Kyla the last.

Thwup, thwup.

Thwup.

"Moving," Matt said.

Kyla followed.

The assassins removed their gas masks, tossed them aside, cleared the false doorway, took up tactical positions on the open steel balcony overlooking the massive facility, dropped low, spied two additional guards as they ran towards the foot of the metal staircase, dispatched them accordingly, then quickly descended the stairs into the lab.

Matt pushed the Sig's sound suppressor into the chest of the first fallen sentry. "Forsythe," he said. "Where is he?"

The man clutched at Matt's weapon as he fought to breathe, tried to push it away.

"*Where?*" Matt repeated.

The man exhaled slowly. His hand fell away from the weapon. He stared up at Matt, dead.

The round came out of nowhere. Kyla cried out, fell back, grabbed her arm.

"Kyla!" Matt yelled. He looked up, saw the figure in the distance, watched him race across the back of the lab, then disappear out of sight. Caucasian. Blue blazer. Black dress pants. White shirt. Dress shoes.

It had to be Forsythe.

Matt turned his attention back to Kyla, pushed her hand away from her arm. "How bad is it?" he asked.

"It's just a scratch," Kyla replied. "I'll be fine. Find that mother and take him out." She forced a smile. "Just another day at the office, remember?"

Matt winked. "Beautiful and tough. Some girls have it all."

"Don't you ever forget it," Kyla replied. "Now go."

MATT SEARCHED THE FACILITY, called out. "Not a very bright thing to do, firing a gun in a meth lab," he said. "You familiar with the concept of open muzzle flash? You'll blow this place sky high."

The response came from a distant part of the lab. "Who are you?"

"Someone you pissed off."

The man's voice reverberated off the walls and ceiling. "You wouldn't be the first."

Matt circled the vats and equipment, responded. "Yeah, but I'll definitely be the last."

"I wouldn't count on it."

The second round whizzed past Matt's head, pinged off a metal supplies rack, ricocheted, shattered a large glass flask.

The man called out. "Maybe we can discuss this, find some common ground. What do you think?"

"I think I'd rather kill you."

"Shame. I could make you a very rich man."

"Who says I'm not?"

"Trust me, pal. You're not my kind of rich."

"I saw your car when you pulled in. Not bad."

"You want it? No problem. I'll toss you the keys."

"I'll pass."

"You going to tell me why you're here?"

"You messed with my friends. Big mistake."

"Who might they be?"

"Domenic Vitagliano and his family."

"The old man who runs the mission?"

"Not runs. *Ran.* You had it firebombed, remember?"

"I have no idea what you're talking about."

Matt slipped quietly around the corner, touched the Sig's suppressor against the back of David Forsythe's head. "Yeah, you do," he said. "You know exactly what I'm talking about. Now drop the gun."

Forsythe hesitated, tried to turn.

Matt drew back the Sig, slammed it hard into the side of

Forsythe's head, then pressed the muzzle against the back of his skull. "Go on," he said. "Give me a reason."

Forsythe dropped the weapon.

Matt kicked it under a nearby supply rack.

Forsythe recovered from the blow, groaned. "How's your partner? Dead, I hope."

"From one bullet?" Matt said. "All that did was piss her off. Now move."

"Where are we going?"

"You'll see."

MATT WALKED the drug dealer from the back of the super lab to the foot of the staircase where Kyla was now standing.

"That's him?" she asked.

Matt nodded.

"Doesn't look like much, does he?"

Matt smiled. "I didn't think so either."

Forsythe looked Kyla up and down. "Damn, you're hot. How's the arm?"

"Not as bad as your face."

Forsythe smiled, looked at Matt. "It's still not too late to take me up on my offer. Name your price. Five million? Ten?"

"Gee, Matt," Kyla said. "Think he'll go to twenty?"

"Twenty million?" Forsythe said. "Done. Give me an account number. I'll transfer it to you right now."

Kyla shook her head. "No, thanks." She paused. "There is one thing you could do for me, however."

"Name it."

"I'm going to make a phone call and keep it on speaker.

I'll whisper in your ear and tell you exactly what to say. If you say anything other than what I tell you, my friend here will put a bullet in your brain. Understand?"

"What's in it for me?"

"You get to live."

"Sounds reasonable."

Kyla removed Badger's phone from her pocket, powered it up, removed the assassin's severed thumb from her pocket, pressed it against the biometric login pad. The screen illuminated. She turned to Forsythe. "Ready?"

At the sight of the severed digit, the drug dealer swallowed hard, nodded.

Kyla selected a number she recognized from Badger's call log, pressed SEND.

The call was answered immediately. "Ferriman."

Forsythe listened to Kyla's voice in his ear, repeated what she told him word for word. "It's done," he said. "Reaper has been terminated. Standing down on Alpha One Protocol."

"Good work," Ferriman replied. "What about Reese?"

"She got in the way. Collateral damage. It was necessary."

Ferriman paused. "Very well. Are you still in New York?"

"Yes."

"Stay there. We've picked up chatter. We may need you again soon."

"Copy that."

Ferriman terminated the call, as did Kyla.

Kyla stepped aside, smiled. "You did great," she did. "I'm impressed."

"I agree," Matt said. "That was an outstanding performance."

Forsythe stared at Matt. "I recognize you," he said. "One

of my guys sent me a video. You're the one who beat the shit out of my men."

"It wasn't hard."

Forsythe smiled. "I'm not surprised. Good help is so hard to find these days. So, what happens now?"

Matt shook his head. "Nothing." He placed the Sig's muzzle against Forsythe's head, pulled the trigger.

The drug dealer dropped dead at his feet.

Matt stepped over the dead man, headed for the stairs. "Come on," he said. "I have a couple of things to do before we leave New York, starting with this place."

Kyla followed. "Right behind you."

"LEAVE THE DOOR OPEN BEHIND YOU," Matt said when they reached the top of the stairs and exited the super lab.

Kyla held open the lab's false door with boxes of fireworks she retrieved from the shelves. "Now what?" she asked.

"Give me a minute."

Matt scoured the shelves, found a box labeled LONG DISTANCE REMOTE CONTROL FIREWORK IGNITOR SYSTEM, tore open the package, removed its contents. He opened the back panel of the two channel handheld wireless remote controlled transmitter, inserted the provided batteries, pressed the power button, tested it. The LED glowed green. The device was functional. Next, he pillaged several more boxes, removed their ignitors. From the last box, he removed the system's external antenna. The instructions confirmed the systems working distance from transmitter to receiver to be 6,000 feet.

This would do perfectly.

Kyla watched him assemble the device. "What do you have in mind?" she asked.

"This is a fireworks distribution company, right?" Matt replied.

"That it is."

"Then let's give the city a show it won't soon forget."

Matt pulled a box labelled 1.3G **HIGH LEVEL DISPLAY FIREWORKS** from the shelf, then reentered the lab. He removed a firework from the box, inserted an ignitor into one end of the commercial grade explosive, then moved throughout the lab opening bottles of acetone, pseudoephedrine, anhydrous ammonia, red phosphorus, hydriodic acid, sodium hydroxide, sulphuric acid, iodide crystals, and phenylpropanolamine. The odor emitted by the airborne chemical gases was noxious. Matt held his breath, ran up the stairs, exited the lab, left open the equipment cabinet door that served as the false entrance to the Sapphire Slam methamphetamine production facility.

As Kyla tore open boxes of fireworks, cracked them in half, and scatted their contents loosely over the warehouse floor, Matt set up two additional firework/ignitor stations, one in the north end of the warehouse, the second in the south end.

They had finished rigging the building.

"Time to go," Matt said.

"Where to?" Kyla asked.

"The Vitagliano's."

53

Just Say Yes

DOMENIC HEARD THE knock on his front door, answered it, found his new friends standing on his doorstep. "Matt, Kyla," he said. "Please, come in."

Matt and Kyla stepped inside.

"Are you two all right?" he asked.

Matt nodded. "Never better."

Domenic hesitated. "And Forsythe?"

"You and your family won't have to worry about him anymore."

"Is he...?"

"Very."

Matt saw the look of concern on his friend's face. "Never mind, Domenic," he said. "There's nothing to tie Forsythe's termination to you whatsoever."

Domenic pondered the word, repeated it. "Termination. That sounds so... final."

"It is," Matt said.

"It also sounds like something a professional would say. An assassin, perhaps."

Matt smiled. "It's best that you continue to know as little about me as possible."

"I take it that applies to Kyla as well?"

Kyla smiled. "Yes, Mr. Vitagliano," she said. "It does."

Domenic looked out his door, stared at the signage on Matt's van parked in front of his house. "One thing's for certain," he said.

"What's that?" Matt asked.

"You're not in the window cleaning business."

Matt shook his head. "No, I'm not."

Carla and Francesca joined Domenic in the vestibule. They hugged Matt and Kyla. "Please stay with us for a while," Carla said.

"Thank you," Matt said, "but I'm afraid that's not possible. We have to be on our way."

"I understand," Domenic said. "Is there anything we can do for you before you go?"

Matt nodded. "Yes, there is."

"Name it."

"I have two stops to make. I need you to come with me."

"Of course," Domenic replied. "Where are we going?"

"The Block B apartment complex. There are a couple of people I want to see there."

Domenic nodded. "I'll grab my coat."

"I'll need to ask a favor of you when we get there," Matt said. "It's not for me. It's for someone who could really use your help."

"*My* help?" Domenic asked. "Who is it?"

Matt smiled. "You'll see."

KYLA WAITED with Carla and Francesca while Matt and Domenic visited the Block B apartments. Carla treated the flesh wound to her arm.

"WHAT ARE WE DOING HERE?" Domenic asked as Matt pulled the van into the Visitors parking lot.

"I'd like you to introduce me to your friends," Matt said.

"My friends?"

"Angelina and Cassidy Ruffalo."

Domenic observed members of the Forsythe's gang standing in the driveway of the building blocking the main entranceway. "I don't know, Matt," he said. "This doesn't look like a good time. Maybe we should come back later."

Matt glanced at the men. "Don't worry about them," he said. "They won't bother us."

"How can you be sure?"

Matt opened his door, stepped out of the van. "Just a feeling."

Matt and Domenic walked up the driveway. "Evening, boys," Matt said as they approached the men.

The men recognized Matt from his earlier altercation with their associates. They said nothing, stepped aside, permitted him to enter the building without discussion or confrontation.

Inside the lobby, Domenic turned to Matt. "Do they know you?" he asked.

Matt smiled. "You could say that. Which apartment?"

"712."

Matt pressed the call button, waited for the elevator to arrive. The men took the car to the seventh floor, exited. Domenic knocked on the door.

"Yes?"

"Angelina, it's Domenic Vitagliano."

"Mr. Vitagliano... from the mission?"

"Yes, ma'am."

Angelina cracked open the door, peered out, saw Matt.

Domenic smiled. "It's all right, Angelina. This is my friend, Matt. Would it be all right if we spoke to you for a moment?"

Angelina nodded, opened the door.

Matt and Domenic entered the small apartment.

"I heard about what happened," Domenic said. "How's Cassidy doing?"

Angelina smiled. "We're taking things one day at a time."

"That's good," Domenic said.

"To what do I owe the pleasure?" Angelina asked.

"Actually," Matt said. "I asked Domenic if he would be kind enough to formally introduce me to you."

"Formally?" Angelina said. "I'm sorry, Matt. I don't recognize you. Have we met before?"

"No, ma'am."

Angelina looked puzzled. "I don't understand."

"You were with your daughter in the ICU when I stopped by. I didn't want to disturb you, so I wrote a note and had a nurse deliver it to you."

Angelina stared at Matt, then walked into her kitchen,

retrieved the handwritten note from beneath a butterfly-shaped magnet affixed to her fridge. "You wrote this?" she asked.

Matt nodded. "Yes, ma'am."

Angelina reread the note. "But you don't know me or my daughter."

"No, ma'am. I don't."

"Yet you say you're a friend."

"I'd like to be."

Angelina turned to Domenic. "What's going on?"

Domenic shook his head. "To be honest, I'm not entirely sure myself."

Matt spoke. "Forgive me, Mrs. Ruffalo. I know this might seem strange to you and perhaps somewhat of an intrusion, but I assure you it's not. Simply put, I'm in a position to help you and your daughter. That's precisely what I'd like to do if you would permit me."

"Help us? How?"

"When Cassidy is healthy enough to return home, I'd like to move you out of here and into a new home, one where you'll no longer have to be concerned for your safety."

Angelina shook her head. "We could never afford to move."

"There would be no cost to you whatsoever," Matt said. "Everything will be paid for."

Angelina was speechless. "I'm confused. Why would you do that for someone you don't even know?"

"Because I can, and because it's the right thing to do. What was done to your daughter was disgraceful. From what I've been told by Domenic, you've already been through hell and back."

Angelina nodded. "We have. But that's life. Sometimes it doesn't turn out the way you planned."

"You're right," Matt said. "But if you will allow me, I can help start you on a path to a new and brighter future."

"I'm not sure," Angelina said. "This is all so unexpected and, frankly, unreal."

"I understand your apprehension," Matt said. "We don't know each other. You have every right not to trust me, and I wouldn't blame you if you didn't. But I assure you there is no catch. I own a number of properties in Soundview. One is vacant, fully furnished, and available to you right now at no charge if you want it."

Angelina stared at Matt. Her eyes began to water. "I don't know what to say."

Matt smiled. "That's the easy part. Just say yes."

"That's all?"

"That's all."

Angelina smiled. "All right. Yes!"

"Good," Matt said. He handed Angelina the key to the townhouse which neighbored his own, wrote down the address. "I have to leave the city tonight on an urgent personal matter," he said. He turned to Domenic. "Think you can arrange the Ruffalo's move for me? I'll cover the costs."

Domenic smiled. "I'll be happy to."

Angelina hugged Matt. "You have no idea what this means to us," she said. "None whatsoever."

Matt smiled. "Just take care of yourselves."

Angelina wiped away a tear. "We will."

54

Old Dude

MATT AND DOMENIC left Angelina and Cassidy's apartment. "I have one more stop to make," Matt said. "Just down the road."

"In this neighborhood?" Domenic asked.

Matt nodded. "Building C."

"Who do you know there?"

"A kid who needs your help."

"*My* help?"

"Yes."

"Do I know him?"

Matt and Domenic entered the building. "Not yet, but you will in a minute."

Matt knocked on Benny Ortiz's door.

Benny answered. "Well, I'll be damned."

"Nice to see you, too," Matt replied. "Mind if I come in?"

Benny opened the door, pointed down the hall to his room. "You know where to go." He looked at Domenic. "Who's the old dude?"

"*Old dude?*" Domenic said.

"I'd watch my manners if I were you," Matt said, then made the introductions. "Benny, Domenic Vitagliano. Domenic, Benny Ortiz."

"Hey," Benny said. He raised his hand to high five Domenic. "What's up, man?"

Domenic stared at the teen.

Benny dropped his hand. "Whatever."

"First things first," Matt said. "That shit stops now."

"What shit?" Benny asked.

"Disrespecting your elders. It's not 'man.' It's Mr. Vitagliano, or Sir. Got it?"

Domenic crossed his arms, awaited a response.

"Yeah," Benny said. "I got it."

"So, apologize."

"For what?"

"What part of *disrespect* did you not understand?" Matt asked.

Benny sighed, faced Domenic. "Sorry," he said.

Matt pressed. "Sorry..."

"Sorry, Mr. Vitagliano."

"That's better."

"Now that we're all acquainted," Benny said, "you mind telling me what you're doing here?"

"Keeping my word."

"About?"

"You told me you wanted nothing more than to get out of the Diamondback life. Is that still true?"

"One hundred percent."

"Then I'd like you to meet your new employer."

"My what?" Benny asked.

"His what?" Domenic asked.

"Domenic owes me a favor," Matt said. "I'm going to call in that marker right now by asking if he'll give you a job at his restaurant."

Domenic's eyes widened. "This kid... work at Vitagliano's? He's a thug!"

"Was a thug," Matt corrected. "Now he's a teenager who needs a job."

Benny chuffed. "Me, have a real job? Fat chance. Forsythe owns me."

Matt shook his head. "Forsythe doesn't own anyone or anything anymore."

"Are you saying what I think you're saying?"

"I'm saying you're free to move on with your life. Read into that what you will."

"Holy shit."

Matt turned to Domenic. "So, Domenic, what do you think? Do you see something here that you can work with?"

Domenic shrugged. "Maybe." He stared at Benny, looked him up and down. "Are you teachable?"

Benny nodded. "Yeah."

"Excuse me?" Matt's curt, disapproving tone prompted the appropriate response from the teenager.

Benny realized his mistake, straightened up. "Oh, yeah. Sorry. Yes, Mr. Vitagliano. Yes, sir. I am."

Domenic was not yet convinced. "We serve from five p.m. to nine p.m. six days a week. You need to be there an hour before your shift and an hour after it ends. Have you ever waited on tables before?"

Benny shook his head. "No, sir."

"Then I'll partner you with one of my senior staff. You'll learn the business as you go. The base salary is good, plus you'll tip out at the end of the night."

"Tips? Wow! Thank you, sir!"

"One more thing," Domenic continued. "Vitagliano's is a well-established, high-end steakhouse. I demand that all my employees treat our customers with the utmost courtesy and respect at all times."

"I can do that, sir."

"How much do you know about steak?"

Benny grinned. "I know how to eat it."

Domenic couldn't help but force a smile. "All right," he said. "I'm willing to give you a chance, but only because Matt is vouching for you. And I trust him completely."

"I'm grateful for the opportunity, sir. I promise I won't let you down." Benny turned to Matt. "Thank you."

Matt nodded. "You're out of the Diamondbacks now, Benny. This is a once in a lifetime opportunity to take care of yourself and your grandmother legitimately. I hope you'll make the most of it."

"I will, sir." Benny said. He paused. "So, Diamond Dave is really gone, huh?" he asked.

"It's best if you don't ask any more questions about Forsythe. Understand?"

Benny nodded.

Matt extended his hand. "Take care of yourself, Benny. Make Mr. Vitagliano proud. Who knows, maybe you'll open a restaurant of your own one day."

Benny beamed. "Thank you, sir. I will."

55

Burn Everything

MATT RETURNED DOMENIC to his home where Kyla was waiting. The flesh wound she had taken to her arm had been dressed, wrapped in medical gauze.

"How's the wing?" Matt asked.

"Not bad at all," Kyla replied. She lifted her arm, moved it up and down. "I had an excellent nurse."

Carla laughed. "More like I had an excellent patient."

Matt smiled. "It's getting late, Kyla," he said. "We need to leave."

Kyla nodded. "Copy that."

"Where are you going?" Domenic asked.

Matt shook his head. "Sorry, my friend. I can't tell you that."

Domenic nodded. "I understand. Wherever your travels take you, please be safe."

Matt smiled, shook his hand. "Thank you. We will."

Francesca waited with her grandfather and grandmother in the vestibule. She stepped forward, wrapped her arms around Matt. "Thank you for saving my life," she said.

"You're welcome," Matt replied.

"And remember what I said."

"About what?"

Francesca leaned in, whispered in his ear. "The future Mrs. Random Guy won't wait forever."

Matt smiled. "I will."

Carla kissed them both goodbye. "Thank you, Matt," she said. "For everything."

"You're welcome," Matt said. "Take care of Domenic for me. Make sure he stays out of trouble."

Carla laughed. "I will."

———

MATT DROVE to Kyla's hotel, waited while she collected her belongings. Together, they drove to Matt's townhouse. Kyla waited in the van while he rushed inside, only to return moments later with two backpacks, one of which he had filled. He handed the second bag to Kyla.

"This one is yours," he said. "We're traveling light. Just pack clothing, essentials, and weapons. Leave the rest in the van. Anything else we'll buy when we get to Honduras."

Kyla nodded. "Sounds like a plan."

Matt checked his watch. 11:00 P.M.

Time to go.

MATT REACHED Red Thunder Fireworks and Special Effects at 11:45 P.M., drove the van to the back of the warehouse, backed it up to the receiving dock, removed the wireless remote-control transmitter from the glove box, slipped it into his jacket pocket. As Kyla exited the van, he opened its rear cargo doors. "I'm really going to miss this van," he said.

Kyla smiled. "Yeah, but you know the drill."

Matt nodded. He unscrewed the cap from the emergency gasoline container he kept in the van, emptied its contents over the floor, and splashed down the vehicle's interior and dash. "Burn everything," he replied.

"Afraid so."

TOGETHER THEY LEFT THE VAN, walked along the waterfront to Barretto Point Park. In the distance, a fishing boat approached the Tiffany Street Pier.

Kyla and Matt read the name stenciled across its transom: *Off The Hook.*

Oleg Schroeder stood at the back of the boat. He smiled and waved.

"Our ride's here," Kyla said.

As soon as Matt and Kyla boarded the boat, the captain pulled away from the dock.

Oleg hugged Kyla. "So good to see you again, my dear," he said.

"Same here," Kyla said. "I'm glad you could accommodate my last-minute request. It must have been difficult."

Oleg laughed. "Nothing money cannot solve." He opened his jacket pocket. "Here," he said. "Gifts for you both. Passports and miscellaneous identification as requested, plus all necessary vaccination documents. I also took the liberty of including a little walking around money should you need it, both in American Dollars and Honduran Lempira."

"Thank you," Kyla said.

Matt accepted his envelope from Oleg, put it in his jacket pocket. "I'll need you to do something for me," he said.

"Of course," Oleg said.

"Tell me when we're five thousand feet from shore."

Oleg looked at Matt quizzically. "An odd request, but one I'll be happy to accommodate."

"One more thing."

"What's that?"

"When we reach that position keep going, no matter what happens."

Oleg nodded. "Will do."

MATT AND KYLA stood at the stern of the fishing boat, watched the shoreline fall away.

Moments later, Oleg called down from the captain's chair. "Five thousand feet."

Matt removed the wireless transmitter from his pocket, armed the device. Its green light flashed. He looked at Kyla. "You want to do the honors?"

Kyla smiled, placed her thumb over Matt's. "Let's do it together."

Matt nodded. "For Domenic, Carla, and Francesca."

"For the Vitagliano's," Kyla said.

Together they pressed the button.

Transmitter to antenna.

Antenna to detonators.

Detonators to fuses.

Fuses to fireworks.

The connections were made, the signal complete.

In the distance, the explosion from the hundreds of boxes of combustible inventory stacked on the warehouse shelves and the firework gunpowder Kyla had scattered across the floor blew out the windows of Red Thunder. Seconds later, the building itself erupted into a massive fireball as the exposed gas vapors from the crystal meth lab in its sub-basement found the flame. Behind the building, Matt's gasoline drenched van exploded. He watched as the concussion lifted it high into the air, then fell to the ground, an incinerated heap of cremated metal. Inside, the armaments locker behind the front seat exploded.

It was over. David Forsythe and Sapphire Slam were no more.

Oleg turned the boat towards open water. One hour later, they reached the waiting go-fast boat.

Matt and Kyla thanked Oleg, boarded the craft.

Soon they would reach the cargo vessel *Goliath*.

From there, Honduras awaited.

And freedom.

56
_____

Last Words

ONE DAY LATER

CENTRAL INTELLIGENCE AGENCY
LANGLEY, VIRGINIA

FERRIMAN HEARD the knock on his office door. "Yes?"

The young communications clerk entered the room. "Sir," she said nervously, "I believe we have a problem."

"I have a meeting with Task Force Chief Cross in five minutes," he replied. "Can it wait?"

"No, sir. I don't believe it can."

The director looked up, checked the clock on his office wall, glanced at her ID badge. "This better be good, Bennett."

Bennett set her computer down on Ferriman's desk. "It concerns an audio transmission you received yesterday. Our system has flagged it."

"Meaning?"

"Our software detected a voiceprint anomaly."

"Lose the geek speak. Spell it out for me."

"Yesterday evening, you received a call through an operative's encrypted phone."

Ferriman nodded. "I did. What about it?"

"That device is assigned to Peter Hanson, code name Badger. Records indicate he was assigned an Alpha One Priority package. The target was Matt Gamble, code name Reaper."

"That's correct."

"When was the last time you spoke to Hanson, sir?"

Ferriman shook his head. "Until yesterday? Never."

"Never?"

"No. Why would I? He's just a file number to me. One of dozens of assets I have at my disposal."

Bennett nodded. "That explains why you didn't know."

"Didn't know what?"

The communications clerk tapped on her keyboard, brought up a split screen. "It's best if I show you. As you know, we maintain a library of biometric voice data files on all of our field operatives for verification purposes."

"So?"

The clerk slid her finger across the laptop's trackpad, played Ferriman the recorded call. "Watch the screen, sir."

As the audio file played, the signal on the top half of the

screen differed significantly from the signal on the bottom half.

"What am I looking at?" Ferriman asked.

"Badger's call to you. Everything about it is wrong. The predictive and phonetic codes don't match, nor do the accent, tone, speed of vocal delivery, inflection, pitch, or articulation. The bottom line is this. The caller's voice matches neither Badger's tuning baseline nor the algorithmic voiceprint we established for him."

"Meaning?"

"I don't know who you were talking to, sir, but it wasn't Badger."

Ferriman felt the blood run out of his face. "Are you sure about this?"

The communications clerk nodded. "One hundred percent. That's the thing about data, sir. It doesn't lie. And there is one more thing."

"What?"

"We've been attempting to reach Badger since the discrepancy was discovered. He's not picking up."

Ferriman leaned back in his chair, contemplated the gravity of the situation and what it truly meant. "Who else knows about this?"

Bennett shook her head. "No one, sir. I felt it was best to bring it to your attention first."

"You did the right thing."

"Thank you."

"You need to do me a favor."

"Of course."

"Keep this quiet for the moment. I need to figure out how best to handle this."

"Yes, sir."

"That will be all."

Bennett took the hint, closed her laptop, left Ferriman's office.

Cross was expecting him. As far as he was concerned, the matter with Reaper had been settled. Badger had terminated him.

Ferriman now knew this was not the case.

The call had been faked. Which meant Reaper was most likely still alive.

He opened his computer, pulled up his field asset directory, searched a name: REESE, KYLA. He called her number.

Voicemail.

There was only one logical explanation. "Jesus," he said aloud. "Reaper and Reese are together."

His desk phone rang. The display read **CROSS**.

The Task Force Chief was expecting him. The entire operation had gone sideways. On his watch.

There was one last action he could take, one that would save his ass and bring the matter to a close once and for all.

He picked up the phone, placed a call.

"Strategic Services. Quint speaking."

"This is Ferriman."

"Yes, Director."

"I need to issue an agency alert."

"Target identification?"

"Sending the files now."

Quint waited. "Received, sir," he said. "Two target packages. Matt Gamble and Kyla Reese. Level?"

"Alpha One Priority, Capture/Kill."

"Sir, we already have an active A1P C/K on Gamble."

"I know. Expand the order to include Reese."

"Geographic restrictions on the targets?"

"None. Make it global."

"Yes, sir."

Ferriman terminated the call. He stared at the phone, then remembered his last words to Matt. *'The world is a small place, especially for us. There's nowhere you'll be able to hide. We will find you.'*

That theory was about to be put to the test.

ALSO BY GARY WINSTON BROWN

MATT GAMBLE ACTION THRILLER SERIES

Good As Dead (Book 1)

Devil's Road (Book 2)

NOMAD (Book 3)

JORDAN QUEST FBI PSYCHIC THRILLER SERIES

Intruders (Book 1)

The Sin Keeper (Book 2)

Mr. Grimm (Book 3)

Nine Lives (Book 4)

Live To Tell (Book 5)

Nemesis (Book 6)

Tiny Bones (Book 7)

Old Ghosts (Book 8)

The Bad Man (Book 9)

Two Graves (coming soon)

Jordan Quest Digital Boxset 1 (Intruders, The Sin Keeper, Mr. Grimm)

Jordan Quest Digital Boxset 2 (Nine Lives, Live To Tell, Nemesis)

Jordan Quest Digital Boxset 3 (Tiny Bones, Old Ghosts, The Bad Man)

STANDALONE THRILLERS

The Vanishing

ABOUT THE AUTHOR

Gary Winston Brown is the author of the Jordan Quest FBI Psychic Thriller series and Matt Gamble Action Thriller series. He lives just outside Toronto, Canada.

If you enjoyed reading **GOOD AS DEAD**, kindly rate and review it on Amazon!

f ⊙ a

JOIN GARY'S READERS CLUB

Want to be kept up to date on new release and preorder announcements, special offers (like signed paperback draws), and more ? It's easy. Visit my website to subscribe to my no-spam-ever newsletter and receive a free book!

GaryWinstonBrown.com

You can unsubscribe at any time, but I hope you'll stick around.

Printed in Dunstable, United Kingdom